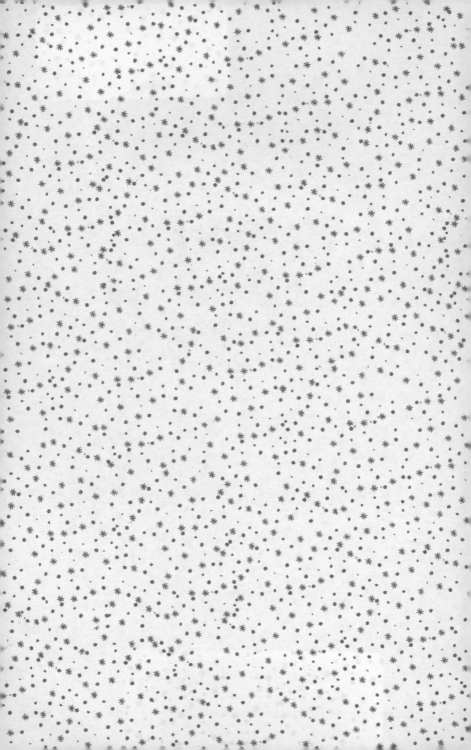

GABRIEL
and the
Phantom
Sleepers

Books by Jenny Nimmo

Midnight for Charlie Bone
Charlie Bone and the Time Twister
Charlie Bone and the Blue Boa
Charlie Bone and the Castle of Mirrors
Charlie Bone and the Hidden King
Charlie Bone and the Wilderness Wolf
Charlie Bone and the Shadow of Badlock
Charlie Bone and the Red Knight

Henry and the Guardians of the Lost

The Secret Kingdom
The Secret Kingdom: The Stones of Ravenglass
The Secret Kingdom: Leopard's Gold

The Snow Spider (Modern Classics edition)
The Snow Spider Trilogy

GABRIEL
and the
Phantom
Sleepers

JENNY NIMMO

EGMONT

EGMONT

We bring stories to life

First published in paperback in Great Britain 2018
by Egmont UK Limited
The Yellow Building, 1 Nicholas Road, London W11 4AN

Text copyright © 2018 Jenny Nimmo
Cover illustration by George Ermos

The moral rights of the author and illustrator have been asserted

ISBN 978 1 4052 8088 4

www.egmont.co.uk

63341/001

A CIP catalogue record for this title is available from the British Library

Typeset by Avon DataSet Ltd, Bidford on Avon, Warwickshire
Printed and bound by in Great Britain by the CPI Group

Stay safe online. Any website addresses listed in this book are correct
at the time of going to print. However, Egmont is not responsible for content
hosted by third parties. Please be aware that online content can be subject
to change and websites can contain content that is unsuitable for children.
We advise that all children are supervised when using the internet.

Egmont takes its responsibility to the planet and its inhabitants very seriously.
We aim to use papers from well-managed forests run by responsible suppliers.

For Rhiannon and Seren, with love.

CONTENTS

PROLOGUE

At the age of three Cecily Fork cast her first spell. She turned a kitten into a toad. Her horrified parents decided to keep quiet about it. They persuaded Cecily never to cast her spells in public and she agreed. After all, keeping her sorcery a secret was much more fun. No one ever guessed who had turned the neighbourhood dogs into monkeys, or caused popular girls to grow carrot noses, and Cecily pretended to be as surprised as anyone when pencils turned into slugs and books became white rats.

When Cecily was eighteen she left her nice, ordinary parents and went to live with more exciting Fork relatives. They were treacherous villains with large ears and dreadful habits. They adored Cecily and would do anything for her, however cruel or unlawful.

In her twenties Cecily enchanted two rich men into marrying her – one by one, of course. The marriages didn't work out, but by then Cecily had two sons, one from each marriage; Carver and Septimus. When Carver was eight and Septimus was six, Cecily heard about a certain magical cloak. The cloak was a thousand years old and had once belonged to an African magician, the so-called Red King. It was made by a forest jinni from the web of the last moon spider, and it could protect the wearer from any curse, weapon or spell.

The king turned the web into a cloak, the deep red colour of the setting sun. He left his fabulous garment in the care of the Silk family, and the oldest member of every Silk generation inherited the duties of keeping the cloak secret and safe. Oh, how Cecily longed for that cloak; it would strengthen her power and make her invincible.

Once again Cecily used a spell to captivate a husband. This time it was Jack Silk, who was expected to inherit the cloak from his elderly father. The wicked Forks carried out a plan to get rid of Jack's first wife, and then Cecily and the unfortunate, enchanted Jack were married. Cecily waited, biding her time until the cloak fell into her hands. But Jack's twin brother, Alan, became Keeper of the Cloak instead, and Cecily could hardly contain her fury. Punishing Jack with a spell that imprisoned him in his house forever, she departed, leaving Jack utterly mystified and his daughter, Sadie, elated. Cecily had been a cruel stepmother.

No one knew why Cecily had married Jack. The Silk family never guessed that Cecily had heard about the cloak and yearned for it. Perhaps no one would ever have found out, if Gabriel Silk hadn't become Keeper of the Cloak for one exceedingly dangerous week.

CHAPTER ONE
The Hooded Stranger

The invitation sat on a shelf above the kitchen stove. It was edged in red and gold, and printed in an ornate, ancient-looking script. It said:

'You are honoured to receive this invitation to:
A fantastical convention of the alchemists' society.'

At the bottom of the card in small print was a date and the name of an obscure town in Belgium.

Mr Silk's name was handwritten at the top, and he was forever looking at it and smiling to himself. The rest of the family tried to ignore it, especially Mrs Silk, she couldn't be doing with alchemy or any other fantastical activity. She put up with her son, Gabriel's, seventh sense only as long as it didn't affect his three sisters.

Gabriel was secretly pleased about the invitation, but also a little nervous, for it meant that, while his father was away, he would be Keeper of the king's cloak for a whole week.

Mrs Silk had made a firm promise to take her three daughters to visit their cousins, but Gabriel wanted to stay with his Uncle Jack and cousin Sadie instead. There was simply no room for him at his Aunt's place.

The cloak couldn't be left in an empty house, so it was decided that Gabriel was the best person to take charge of it. After all, no one would believe that a mere boy would be in possession of such a garment.

Today there was chaos in the Silk household. The girls were upstairs preparing for their holiday. There were arguments over clothes, bags of toys, shoes (lost and then found), crisps, car-seats and even bananas. Sylvie was eight and Sally a year younger. Bonnie was five and had the loudest voice. Gabriel was twelve.

'You can still change your mind,' Mrs Silk told Gabriel.

Gabriel grinned and shook his head.

'I don't like to think of you going all that way with the cloak,' went on Mrs Silk, 'but I promised my sister I would visit, and the girls are dying to see their cousins.'

Alice and Annie were the same age as Sylvie and Sally.

'There wouldn't be room for me,' said Gabriel, 'and anyway Dad's friend Albert will be travelling with me, all the way.'

Mrs Silk sighed. 'If only Dad didn't have to go to this wretched convention. He's not even an alchemist.'

Gabriel rolled his eyes. 'But it's an honour, and he'll get loads of ideas for his books.'

'So he says,' muttered his mother, tight-lipped.

Sylvie burst into the kitchen, waving a pink bag. 'We're ready,' she cried.

Gabriel and his mother went out to the car. Arguments over, the girls were waiting happily beside it. After many hugs and wet kisses, Gabriel and his father watched the girls pile into the car. There was a loud toot, much waving and then Mrs Silk's car was bumping down the muddy lane.

It was time for Gabriel to begin his own journey. But first – the cloak. He followed his father upstairs. Mr Silk had already taken the cloak from its hiding place in the attic. It was lying on Gabriel's bed. The cloak might have been a thousand years old, but its original bright crimson had hardly faded, and when Gabriel half-closed his eyes he could see tiny stars glittering on the hem. No harm could ever come to the wearer of this garment, but as it was such a priceless treasure the Silks had to keep it as safe and secret as they could.

Mr Silk folded the cloak and rolled it in an old jacket. He placed the jacket on top of a thick sweater in Gabriel's travelling bag and zipped it up. 'Albert will keep an eye on things,' he said cheerily, 'and when you get to Uncle Jack's the cloak will be quite safe. Your uncle never leaves the house.'

'Poor Uncle Jack,' said Gabriel.

'Wicked woman,' muttered Mr Silk, referring to his brother's ex-wife, 'leaving him under such a monstrous spell.'

'D'you think she'll come back?' asked Gabriel.

'Not a chance,' said his father.

'Sadie said she was living in a Russian castle, the last time they heard.'

'There you are then. Come on, Gabriel. Have you got everything you need?'

Gabriel eyed his bag. 'I hope it won't be stolen on the train.'

'There's no fear of that.' Mr Silk patted his son's shoulder. 'Very few people outside the family know about the cloak. Albert knows, of course, but he's my oldest friend.'

'Charlie Bone knows, and Tancred and Emma, and all my friends at Bloor's Academy.'

'They *are* family,' said Mr Silk. 'They're the Red King's descendants, too.'

'Are you sure you don't want to take the cloak

to Belgium with you?' Gabriel asked.

'To an alchemists' convention?' Mr Silk shook his head. 'It'll be crowded with sorcerers and their like. They'd sniff it out in no time.'

'You said that very few people can wear the cloak safely.'

'Indeed,' said Mr Silk. 'But who knows if this applies to sorcerers. Come on, let's get you to the station. I've got a plane to catch when I've seen you off.'

Gabriel picked up his bag and followed his father downstairs. In the hall he shrugged himself into his anorak, while Mr Silk put on a grey woollen coat. It made him look far more important than he usually did. He was a small man, with thinning, sandy hair, mild grey eyes and rimless spectacles.

Gabriel didn't resemble his father in the least. He was tall for his age, lanky and dark. His hair had a habit of flopping over one eye and Gabriel was happy to leave it that way.

When Mr Silk opened the front door the mistletoe over his head swung wildly in a cold breeze. It was only three days after Christmas.

The train station was quiet, their platform deserted. But on the other side of the rails a few passengers stamped up and down, trying to keep warm. All were travelling south.

A blast of freezing air bowled dust and paper down the platform. Wind from the north, where Uncle Jack and Sadie lived. Gabriel turned up his collar. Soon he would be travelling into the mountains and the icy home of the north wind. But Sadie would be there, cooking wonderful things to eat.

Ten minutes passed.

Mr Silk kept staring at his watch. He was beginning to look anxious. 'Train's late,' he muttered. He paced up and down the platform, his hands in his pockets, whistling. There was a note of unease in the whistles. 'The train can't have gone through already,' he said. 'We were here in good time.'

'Perhaps it's been cancelled,' Gabriel suggested.

His father looked even more worried. 'No, no, impossible. I've got to go soon, Gabe. I must get to the airport in time.'

Another ten minutes passed. Mr Silk took out his mobile and called a number. 'Ugh. I'm not getting through,' he said. 'They're probably in a tunnel.'

A few minutes later his phone rang. He pulled it out of his pocket and held it to his ear. 'Albert!' he said. Scattered sounds came from the mobile and Mr Silk replied, 'Great! Sorry to miss you, but Gabriel's here, all ready with the –' he glanced over his shoulder – 'you know what.' After another short burst of sound, Mr Silk said, 'Good! Good! Catch you in the new year, Albert. Thanks for this.'

'Is your friend . . .?'

'He's on the train, but he got the time wrong. It'll be another fifteen minutes, and I must dash, Gabe, or I'll miss my plane.'

'Aren't you going to –' Gabriel began.

'Sorry, son, I've got to go. Albert's nearly here. You'll remember him when you see him. Big man, white moustache. He's going to be wearing a black hat. My oldest friend. You'll be fine.'

'I'll be fine,' Gabriel repeated. He wished the phrase didn't have a whiff of bad luck about it. 'Bye, Dad. Have a good convention.'

'I will. Bye, Gabe.' Mr Silk patted his son's shoulder and walked briskly to the exit. He gave a quick wave and left the station.

Gabriel clutched his bag. He looked over his shoulder, then up and down the platform. A woman in a red coat was now sitting on a bench quite close to him. Gabriel thought she had been staring at him. She quickly glanced away.

The minutes ticked by. Gabriel kept consulting his watch. He had never known fifteen minutes to last so long. On a sudden impulse, he pulled out his phone and rang his friend, Charlie. There was no reply. Gabriel remembered that Charlie was in some far off place with his cousin, Henry. He tried Tancred

Thorsson's number.

'Hi, Gabe,' came Tancred's cheerful voice. 'How –' His next words were drowned by an explosive sneeze in the background. 'Dad's got a cold,' Tancred explained. Gabriel could hear things hitting the floor – tins, perhaps, or knives – and then the smash and tinkle of glass. 'Another window's gone,' said Tancred calmly. In the Thorssons' house it was an almost everyday occurrence.

Tancred and his father were weather-mongers, they could muster up wind, rain, hurricanes, thunder and lightning at will. The trouble was that these powerful elements could also arrive unbidden, especially if the Thorssons were anxious or unwell.

'Are you OK, Gabe?' asked Tancred when the noise had died down.

'I'm OK,' said Gabriel. 'Are you?'

'Yes, yes. I'm fine,' Tancred replied, and then he sneezed.

'Bless you,' said Gabriel. 'Oh, I think I can see the train.'

'OK, Gabe. Bye, then. Have a great time in the north.'

Gabriel was reluctant to let his friend go, but the train was drawing closer. Gabriel hardly had time to get his mobile into a pocket, before three carriages squealed past him into the station. A man leaned out of a window several doors down. He wore a black fur hat.

'Gabriel!' called the man. 'Gabriel Silk?'

'Yes. That's me.' Gabriel picked up his bag and raced towards the figure in the black hat.

The door opened and a large man stepped down on to the platform. 'Hurry, hurry, Gabriel.' The man had a white moustache and wore a grey tweed coat with a black fur collar. Tufts of white hair stuck out from under his hat.

'Good to meet you, Gabriel,' said Albert when Gabriel had reached him. 'I'm Albert Blackstaff.' He gripped Gabriel's free hand, shook it heartily and climbed back into the train. Gabriel leapt up the steps after him.

Albert led the way to a seat with a table. There were only two or three others in the carriage, and then the woman in the red coat came in. She looked at Gabriel who quickly shuffled away from her gaze and towards a window seat. He lifted his bag on to the table and sat behind it. Albert took the seat opposite and winked at him. 'Precious cargo,' he whispered.

'Yes.' Gabriel nodded. He felt foolish because surely no one had followed him, and who was there to steal the bag? Surely not the woman in the red coat.

It was a long journey. Gabriel had been prepared

for that, but he found his companion's silence a bit disturbing. Gabriel had expected him to be a bit more chatty. Almost as soon as they sat down Albert produced a newspaper, shook it out and held it up before him.

Gabriel read his book, an adventure involving pirates and parrots. When he was tired of that, he pulled a bag of sandwiches out of his pocket. They were slightly squashed but still fresh, and Gabriel thought them worth offering.

'Have a sandwich,' he said, holding the bag out to Albert.

The big man shook his paper and peered round the side of it. 'What?'

'Sandwich?' said Gabriel. 'Cheese and tomato, Mum made them.'

'Ah.' Albert eyed the sandwiches and frowned. 'No thanks, Gabriel. I'll wait.' He took off his fur hat, revealing a mop of thick white hair. 'Getting a bit hot in here.'

'Are you going to Meldon as well? I forgot to ask Dad.'

'No, not Meldon.' Albert obviously thought that was enough information.

Gabriel tried to start another conversation. 'Dad says we met when I was five, but I can't really remember.'

'Oh, I can, Gabriel. You were a very bonny little lad.'

'I must have changed a lot.' Gabriel hadn't meant to sound surprised, but he knew he had been anything but a bonny little lad.

'We all change,' Albert said cheerfully. 'Get on well with your Uncle Jack, do you?'

'He's OK.' Gabriel didn't like to mention his uncle's problem. 'My cousin Sadie's great. She can cook anything.'

'Anything?' Albert raised an eyebrow.

'Well, almost anything,' Gabriel amended.

'Ah.' Albert disappeared behind his newspaper again.

Gabriel ate a sandwich and went back to his book.

It began to get dark. In the weak light Gabriel could see winter trees swaying in a fierce north wind.

'Looks cold out there,' he muttered.

'Mm?' Albert lowered his paper and, giving Gabriel a friendly smile, said, 'Get me some tea, would you, Gabriel? Milk, no sugar. And a cake, anything chocolate. And something for yourself, here.' He felt in his pocket and produced a ten pound note. 'Get what you want.' He winked.

Surprised by a second wink, Gabriel took the note and made his way to the restaurant car. He ordered two chocolate muffins, a tea and an orange juice.

While he was waiting, the woman in the red coat came in and stood behind him. 'Be careful,' she said.

Gabriel thought she was warning him not to spill the tea. He was making his way back to his seat, and just crossing the gap between coaches, when suddenly a man leapt in front of him. Where he had come from Gabriel couldn't guess. He recoiled from the man's awful smell, almost dropping his tray. The stranger wore a long, hooded cloak, his pale eyes bulged out of leathery-looking skin and his wrinkled cheeks hung over his jaws like shrivelled balloons.

'Fool!' spat the man. 'Do thy duty.'

'Gabriel was too shocked to move. 'Wha . . .? he mumbled.

'Dost thou forget thou art Keeper?' grunted the apparition.

'No . . . no,' croaked Gabriel.

'Aiee!' cried the hooded man. 'Stop them, or 'twill be the worse for thee.'

'I don't know what you're talking about,' said Gabriel, almost tearfully.

The hooded man growled, showing long cabbage-coloured teeth, but all at once a sharp voice said, 'Leave the boy alone,' and the woman in the red coat strode past Gabriel. She prodded the stranger in the chest, saying, 'Go away. Leave him alone.'

A dreadful sound came from the man. A long,

gasping intake of breath, followed by a snarl. 'I will not harm thee this time, Keeper's friend,' he grunted, 'but beware, I can do worse.' He waved a hand of gnarled, fleshless fingers before the woman's face, then his eyes rolled back into his head, and he vanished.

Gabriel's hands began to shake. The woman in the red coat seemed unable to move. She stared at the space the hooded figure had occupied, her hand still locked on to her cup of tea. Her mouth had dropped open and her eyes were wide and fixed.

'Was . . .? I mean . . . are you?' Gabriel stuttered.

The woman remained in a sort of frozen state, unable to respond in any way, almost as though Gabriel wasn't there.

Gabriel felt he should give her a nudge, or pat her hand, anything to shake her out of her trance, or whatever it was, but he was afraid of spilling Albert's tea. So he just stood beside the woman, who, after all, had saved him from something definitely nasty. 'Er . . . are you?' he said hesitantly. 'No, that's silly, you're definitely not all right, are you?'

'Oh!' The woman gave a long sigh and turned to Gabriel. 'Whatever happened?'

'There was a horrible-looking thing here,' said Gabriel. 'It waved its hand and then it kind of vanished.'

'Of course. How could I forget? You go back to your seat, Gabriel. I'm quite all right now.'

'Are you sure?' Gabriel wondered how she knew his name.

'Yes, yes. But I'm new to the job, and I'd rather you didn't mention my little – er – moment of weakness.' The woman had a warm, friendly smile.

'Who would I mention it to?' asked Gabriel.

'Oh, never mind.' She was quite young, Gabriel reckoned. He thought he'd seen her before somewhere.

'Better get back to your seat,' she said firmly.

Albert appeared to be asleep when Gabriel reached him. Gabriel set the tray in front of the big man, muttering that he was sorry he had taken so long.

Albert opened one eye. 'Muffins,' he said. 'Good choice.'

Gabriel handed over the change and slid into his seat. He thought he should probably mention the hooded stranger, but he waited until Albert had munched his way through his muffin before describing the man who had accosted him.

Albert frowned and placed his cup on the table. 'You should have alerted me before,' he said.

'Sorry. I thought you'd like to finish your tea first,' said Gabriel. 'I hope it's not a bad sign.'

'Who knows?' Albert looked at his watch. 'Ah. Time for my medication,' he said, and he pulled a small travelling bag from under his seat. 'I'll just pop to the toilet, Gabriel. Won't be a tic.'

Gabriel wondered why Albert had to take his bag to the toilet. Perhaps he needed his towel and toothbrush.

Albert was in the toilet for a long time. The train stopped briefly at a station, then rolled on again. Albert still hadn't returned.

Gabriel leaned back in his seat and the train continued into the night. It was now quite dark outside. Gabriel yawned and closed his eyes. Perhaps he fell asleep, he couldn't be sure, but all at once he was aware of the nauseous smell of decay drifting under his nose; the air was thick with it. Gabriel sat up and coughed violently.

There was a faint hoot from the engine and the train began to slow down. Slower and slower. Seconds later it stopped altogether. It was very quiet in the carriage. Gabriel peered through the window. Flurries of snow came floating out of the darkness.

'Snow,' he murmured.

'Fool,' croaked a voice behind him. 'Now it begins.'

CHAPTER TWO
The Sorceress

Earlier that same day, when the sky was still the deep grey of a winter dawn, someone rang Jack Silk's doorbell. Sadie, suddenly wide awake, threw on her dressing gown and ran downstairs, her long pigtail swinging behind her. Gabriel was not expected until the evening, and trains didn't usually arrive this early.

When Sadie opened the front door and found Cecily Fork on the step, she was too stunned to speak. Cecily's son, Septimus, glowered beside her, and the dog, Carver, sat mute on the path. A large shiny car was parked in the road behind them.

Sadie clung to the door to steady herself. The shock took her breath away. 'Oh no,' she mumbled.

'Not very welcoming.' Sadie's ex-stepmother had a voice like a rusty nail scraping the bottom of a saucepan. 'I thought I'd beaten the rudeness out of you.'

'It came back when you left,' said Sadie, feeling more courageous.

Cecily's pale eyes narrowed, Carver snarled and Septimus squawked, 'Stupid girl.'

'What d'you want,' demanded Sadie, still clinging to the door.

The sorceress thrust her aside and strode into the house.

'Dad!' called Sadie.

But he was already standing in the passage, in his dressing gown, his face white with horror.

A breeze smelling of burnt metal followed Cecily into the house. Sadie could feel it pressing about her, numbing her thoughts, muffling sounds. The sorceress, her son and the dog pushed their way into the kitchen, while Sadie and her father followed, helplessly.

Cecily wore a leopard-skin coat, its wide collar cradling her steel grey hair like a bag of knives. 'You don't look pleased to see me,' she grated, staring at Jack.

He didn't reply.

Sadie could see the pain in her father's eyes. It made her want to shout at the sorceress.

Cecily shrugged her shoulders and sat down. 'Do we care if you're pleased?'

'No, we do not,' said Septimus. In his close-fitting grey suit, white shirt and blue tie, he hardly looked like a boy on holiday. He had a round, pink face, and his shiny black hair clung to his head like a skullcap.

Jack sank on to a chair and murmured, 'Why have you come back?'

'Oh, I haven't come back,' said Cecily, drawing off a tight leather glove. You could see the sparkle even before she thrust out her hand. A large emerald glinted on her ring finger. 'I was just passing; had to bring a few Christmas gifts to some friends.'

'Spies, I suppose,' Sadie muttered. 'Some of your relatives keeping an eye on us.'

Cecily ignored her. 'I'm getting married,' she announced, with an unpleasant smile.

'Again?' said Jack.

'Congratulations, you mean,' said Septimus, as he wandered around the kitchen.

Sadie hated the way her ex-stepbrother poked about on counters and shelves. Carver growled and snapped at the boy's ankles and, occasionally, Septimus kicked at the dog, sending him whining under the table. Poor Carver was the result of a spell. He had once been Septimus's older brother, but Cecily had turned him into a dog: a punishment for bullying his little brother. The spell was supposed to last for a day, but it still hadn't worn off.

'Aren't you interested in my future husband?' Cecily asked her third husband.

'Should I be?' asked Jack, with a wobble in his voice.

Septimus leaned over Jack's shoulder and crowed, 'Dr Ichabod Loth of Ludgarth Hall School. He's famous.'

'Indeed.' Jack took a breath. 'Perhaps now is the time for you to set me free, Cecily? I don't know what I did to offend you, but surely my punishment has lasted long enough.'

Cecily raised her eyes to the ceiling, 'Perhaps not,' she said.

Jack folded his arms and stared grimly at the table.

'Dr Ichabod Loth is one of the Hundred Heads,' boasted Septimus. 'They're headmasters of great schools all over the world.'

'We know that,' Sadie muttered. 'We've got friends at Bloor's Academy.'

'They're for gifted children like me,' Septimus went on. 'Weather-mongers, shape-shifters, animal-speakers and stuff. My gift hasn't developed yet, but I've got a lovely voice.'

Cecily smiled fondly at her youngest, and from under the table, Carver gave a forlorn growl.

'Of course, your nephew attends Bloor's Academy,' said Cecily. 'Though I wouldn't call him gifted, poor boy. He has that awful affliction.'

'It's not an affliction,' Sadie burst out. 'It's the

seventh sense. And it's wonderful, because he can feel all sorts of emotions belonging to other people, and he can see what happened to them through their clothes.'

'Huh! Coming to see you, is he?' said Cecily.

Sadie opened her mouth, but nothing came out. Almost in a whisper, her father said, 'How do you know that?'

'As you suggested, I have my spies.' The sorceress carefully pulled her gloves back on and stood up. 'Come along, boys,' she said, drawing the fur over her shoulders. 'It's a long drive to Ludgarth.'

'So you've made it your home already?' Jack said quietly.

'Of course. It suits me very well.' Cecily made for the door, and Septimus marched after her, with Carver snapping at his heels.

Sadie followed, at a distance. When Cecily opened the front door, cold air rushed into the house and Sadie breathed it in gratefully.

The sorceress walked to the gate, her steel-toed boots striking the path like hammers. Sadie pulled the door wider, letting the air flood down the passage and into the kitchen.

Cecily stopped by the gate. 'Aren't you going to close the door, stupid girl?' she said. 'The house will freeze.'

Sadie stared at her ex-stepmother. 'I'm cleansing it,' she said, under her breath.

'What did you say?'

'Mumble, mumble,' Septimus said, sniggering. 'She always mumbled.' He climbed into the back of the huge black vehicle parked before the house. 'Mummy's car goes faster than a jet,' he shouted through the open window.

I bet it does, thought Sadie, it's probably spell-driven.

Cecily remained by the gate. Her small eyes glittered. Sadie's hand went to the place below her neck where a charm lay hidden beneath her sweater.

The sorceress gave a shrill laugh. 'Your fairy star won't protect you forever, Sadie Silk,' she said with a snort.

'Why won't you lift the curse?' Sadie asked gravely.

A cruel smile tilted a corner of Cecily's purple lips. 'Because life isn't perfect,' she retorted.

Sadie stepped back and closed the door.

When she returned to the kitchen she found that her father hadn't moved. He sat at the table, his chin resting on his folded hands, and his grey eyes half-closed. Sadie ran and hugged him. 'Oh, Dad, let's forget her.' Sadie leant her head against his. 'She can't do any worse, and you'll be free, one day, I know you will.'

Her father patted her hand. 'Of course I will. We'll get on with our lives as if Cecily was just a nasty dream.'

Sadie threw back her pigtail and smiled. 'Gabriel's coming, and I'm going to cook a chicken casserole.' She went to the fridge to check on the chicken. 'Phew, it's still there,' she said. 'I thought Cecily might have turned it into a wild boar, just to spite me. I don't know how to cook one of those.'

Her father laughed heartily, and Sadie knew that they would be all right, for a while at least. She spent the next twelve hours cleaning and cooking, and then she put Christmas lights in Gabriel's bedroom. Her father emerged from his workroom for quick snacks and cups of tea, but otherwise he remained tapping, scraping and chiselling. He was making a very impressive table for the Mayor of Meldon.

Just before seven o'clock, Sadie had a wonderful surprise. She had been gazing at the Christmas tree in the window when she saw pale flakes drifting past the street lamp.

'Snow,' she breathed.

Sadie had longed for snow. She loved the way it iced the mountains and brought enchantment to the land.

'You're fanciful like your mother,' her father would say. His voice, slow and gentle when he mentioned his first wife, always brought Sadie closer to the person who had died when she was six, and she would touch the obsidian star, hanging on a gold chain round her neck. It had been a birthday present from her mother; a charm against evil, given in turn to Mrs Silk by a white witch called Alice Angel. It had kept Sadie safe, always, but sadly not her mother, once she had given it away.

To Sadie the whirling crystals seemed to have come especially for her. Her favourite cousin, Gabriel, was on his way to them. He was already on the evening train, and he was carrying the king's cloak.

She went up to the guest room for the tenth time that day, her long pigtail swinging behind her. She plumped up the pillows, straightened the bed cover and went downstairs again. As usual her father was in the big workshop beyond the kitchen. Sadie waited patiently while he tapped a wooden peg in the end of the mayor's table. Jack Silk was a fussy carpenter and hated being interrupted.

'Perhaps I should put some holly in Gabriel's room?' Sadie suggested, when her father had laid aside his mallet.

Mr Silk mopped his forehead with a red handkerchief. 'Why?' he asked.

'Because it's still the Christmas holidays,' said Sadie.

Her father's grey eyes twinkled behind his gold-rimmed spectacles. The lenses were streaked with oil and sawdust. Sadie wondered if he could actually see her. 'So it is,' he said. 'Let's have some of your magnificent fruit cake.'

Sadie beamed with pleasure. 'Gabriel's train is taking a long time.'

Mr Silk consulted his watch. 'He'll be here in less than an hour. I've asked Ned-next-door to meet the train.'

Ned-next-door was the best friend anyone like housebound Jack Silk could have. But whenever Ned helped out, Sadie thought of her stepmother's curse.

While the Silks ate fruit cake, Sadie kept an eye on the clock. She had laid a place for Gabriel, ready for his arrival. Half an hour passed, and then another. At eight o' clock the doorbell rang. Sadie ran to open the front door. Ned stood there, looking serious. Snow fell steadily about him. Sadie took him into the kitchen.

'Train never arrived,' said Ned, pulling off his woolly hat. 'They said at the station that it was held up by snow.'

'Ah, the snow,' said Jack.

'What shall I do? Go back to the station and wait?' Ned didn't look too keen on this idea.

'No, no.' Mr Silk began to pace up and down the

kitchen. 'They'll send a bus. They usually do. We'll just sit tight. You go home, Ned, and thank you.'

But when Ned had gone, Mr Silk began to rub his head, hunch his shoulders and pace even faster. Sadie knew why. Her father was worried about the cloak. Would Gabriel keep it safe? He was known to be a bit dreamy, forgetful even. But Sadie trusted him. He would never let the magic cloak out of his sight, not for a moment. He was the Keeper for a whole week. What an honour!

Sadie had seen the cloak once before. Gabriel's father had brought it to Meldon, hoping it could break Cecily's cruel spell. But it was too late. The cloak had been made as a protection against evil; it could not undo a spell that had already been cast.

And yet . . . and yet . . . Sadie remembered how the cloak had gripped her in its silent power when she touched it. There was such great magic there, and it was coming back to them. Gabriel was on his way. 'I'll ring railway enquiries,' she said. Her father was not a practical man. Someone in the family had to be.

But railway enquiries were out of reach, even on the landline.

'It's the snow,' muttered Mr Silk.

Sadie made another pot of tea, and her father sat down again. But Sadie found herself going to the front door. When she opened it there was no one there. So she stood on the step and gazed at the falling snow. For some reason she felt as she had when she touched the cloak, held in thrall by some wonderful enchantment. It was as if the snow was watching her.

CHAPTER THREE
The Woman in the Red Coat

Gabriel was still on the train. He dared not turn around to see who was behind him. He stared straight ahead, telling himself that there was no one there, no one with such an overpowering stink it made him feel sick. He held his nose and closed his mouth. As long as he didn't see the thing that smelled so bad, as long as he didn't look it in the eye, he hoped that it might just disappear.

But a person can't last forever without taking a breath, and eventually Gabriel had to release his nose. The smell lingered but it was gradually fading. Gabriel stood up and looked along the carriage. It appeared to be empty. Suddenly, above his head, the conductor's voice informed passengers that, due to a fall of snow ahead of them, the train could go no further. However, a bus would arrive within the hour.

Gabriel pulled out his mobile and tried to contact his uncle. There was no signal. 'Of course not,'

Gabriel said with a sigh, 'we're in the wild.'

The door at the end of the carriage opened and the woman in the red coat came in. She walked briskly down the aisle, saying, 'Oh, there you are.'

'The train seems to be stuck,' Gabriel remarked, a little nervously.

'We must get off right now,' she said.

'Must we?' said Gabriel. 'But it's cold outside, and the bus might not arrive for an hour.'

'We're not waiting for a bus,' said the woman.

'Er,' Gabriel said hesitantly, 'my friend hasn't come back from the toilet.'

'If you mean that man with the white moustache,' said the woman, 'he got off at the last station.'

Gabriel gaped at her. 'But he can't have. He never said goodbye.'

'The train probably arrived at his station sooner than he expected. Never mind. Let's get off now.'

'I saw him,' she went on as Gabriel continued to look uncertain. 'I asked him why you weren't with him and he told me to mind my own business. We're getting off now.'

Maybe she had decided to try and escape the hooded man, Gabriel thought. 'OK,' he said.

The woman lifted Gabriel's bag off the table, but he jumped up, crying, 'No. You can't. It's mine.'

'Ssh!' the woman hissed. She handed the bag to

Gabriel. 'I'm sorry, you must be very confused.' She smiled again and said, in a hushed voice, 'I'm Hetty Bean, a friend of Cook's, you know, at Bloor's Academy. She asked me to watch over you, and so I'm what she calls a Guardian now. Please trust me. We must get away from that stinking stranger as soon as we can.'

Gabriel nodded in agreement. 'I think I've seen you in the dining hall at Bloor's.'

Hetty smiled. 'That's me. Cook's assistant – well, apprentice, really.' She picked up Albert's black hat. 'Is this yours?'

'No, it's Albert's, my companion. He must have left it behind.'

Hetty thrust the hat into her pocket. 'Come on, then,' she said, and hurried down the aisle.

Gabriel followed, hugging his bag. Hetty was already opening the train door when he reached her. She stepped down on to the platform and held up a hand to help with the bag. Gabriel clung to it and jumped out. The cold wind wrapped itself round their legs, and flurries of snow drifted into their faces. Gabriel turned his back to the wind and gulped. 'I'm not sure about this.'

Hetty patted his shoulder. 'Everything will be fine. I called my father before we lost signal. He won't be long.'

Gabriel stared at the train. It looked very cosy in there. He couldn't see the hooded stranger in any of the windows. Where was he? And why had Albert got off without saying goodbye? It didn't make sense. Gabriel turned away from the train and looked over the platform railing. Fields of grey snow stretched into the darkness. 'We're nowhere,' he said.

'We're in Humbledown.' Hetty pointed to a sign, halfway down the platform. 'We had to get away from it, Gabriel. Hopefully it doesn't know we got out, but you'd better stand back, out of the light from the windows.'

Gabriel shuffled backwards into the shadows, and Hetty squinted at her watch in the weak beam from a lamp post. 'Come on, Dad,' she muttered.

'Just now, you said IT,' said Gabriel. 'It?'

'You know what I mean,' said Hetty.

Gabriel nodded. 'It smelled like something dead.'

'I think it was, Gabriel.' Hetty grimaced. 'Dead but dangerous.'

Gabriel stared speechlessly at Hetty's friendly face. And then, through the whine of the wind he caught the distinct sound of an engine.

'Here he comes,' said Hetty.

The engine noise was accompanied by a loud crunching sound, and then, between two rows of snow-laden hedges, a large vehicle rolled into view.

'It's a tractor,' said Gabriel. For all that it was decked out in fairy lights, tinsel and holly, there was no denying that the big vehicle in the car park was a tractor.

'Only thing in this weather,' said Hetty. 'Come on!' She dashed to the end of the platform and began to descend the steps.

For a moment, Gabriel found himself gazing at the falling snow. There was something unusual about those elegantly dancing crystals. They seemed to be watching him.

He ran to the end of the platform and down the steps; there he found Hetty embracing a large man in a green boiler suit.

'Gabriel!' Releasing Hetty, the big man grabbed Gabriel's hand and shook it so vigorously Gabriel thought his arm might fall off. 'Fred Bean,' the man said in a rumbly voice. 'Pleased to meet one of the gifted ones, and one with SUCH a big responsibility.'

'It's only for a few days,' said Gabriel, wondering how Fred Bean knew so much.

'Indeed, but what a privilege.'

Unsure as to which of them was privileged, Gabriel allowed himself to be bundled up into the cab of the tractor. Hetty hauled herself after him, and Fred climbed into the driving seat. It was a bit of a squash, but at least they were dry.

The tractor bumped its way round the small parking area and then they were off, down the narrow lane, the snow thickening around them and the large wipers squeaking across the windscreen.

Fred Bean began to sing carols and Hetty explained that her father always did this for at least a month after Christmas. She invited Gabriel to join in. 'Everyone knows a carol,' she said cheerfully. And so they sang their way through the silent countryside with the wind whistling at their backs, and the headlights sweeping across glistening drifts of snow. Gabriel found that he felt completely safe with two people that he really didn't know at all. He even forgot to ask where they were going until he saw the lights of a small town twinkling ahead of them. Behind the town, the lower slopes of a mountain could be seen, before it disappeared up into the dark sky.

'Here we are, Meldon itself,' Fred happily announced.

Gabriel suddenly realised he hadn't told either of his rescuers where he wanted to go. 'How did you know?' he asked Hetty, who was squeezed into his side.

'Cook,' she said. 'You might not have needed us at all, but your father rang her, just in case. And she did the rest.'

They were now rolling along Meldon High Street.

The tractor made a difficult manoeuvre round a corner and then they were driving down a long steep road, with snow piled at the kerbs, and terraced houses with holly wreathes on their brightly painted doors. After the lonely wilderness of the fields, it was a surprise to see Christmas lights still twinkling in windows, and trees festooned with coloured globes and tinsel.

They came, at last, to three older buildings, timber-framed and roofed in lichen-covered slate.

'Number twenty-nine, if I'm not mistaken,' said Fred, bringing the tractor to a grinding halt. 'The Carpenter's Cabin.'

'You knew the number.' This time Gabriel wasn't surprised.

'Dad knows your uncle,' said Hetty, climbing from the cab. 'Jack Silk made him a table.'

'A fine table,' said Fred.

Gabriel thanked Fred for the lift and jumped out. Hetty followed him down the path to the front door, and waited while he rang the doorbell. His uncle's Christmas wreath was hung with strong-smelling cloves and wrinkled tangerines. 'Sadie's work,' Gabriel said with a grin. 'My cousin,' he told Hetty.

The door opened and there was Sadie, with the widest smile Gabriel had seen in a long while.

'Gabriel!' she shrieked and, flinging her arms

round his neck, dragged him into the hall.

'Hold on, Sadie,' Gabriel said through slightly embarrassed giggles.

Sadie caught sight of Hetty, lingering on the doorstep. Releasing Gabriel with a squeak of surprise, she said, 'Who are you?'

'This is Hetty Bean, who rescued me,' said Gabriel. He pointed to the tractor and added, 'And that's her dad, who brought us here!'

In a tractor,' cried Sadie, delightedly. 'Hetty, do you want some tea? And your dad, in the tractor, would he like some?'

Hetty shook her head. 'I'll just come in and make sure Gabriel's safe.'

'Of course he's safe.' Sadie led the way into the kitchen.

Uncle Jack gave Gabriel a hug and shook Hetty's hand, and then Hetty gave a brief account of the stranger on the train, Albert's disappearance and her role in Gabriel's rescue.

Mr Silk looked concerned. 'I don't like the sound of this hooded stranger,' he said. 'What do you mean about his smell?'

Hetty struggled for an answer and Gabriel said, 'He smelled like something rotten, you know, dead.'

'And he knew you were the Keeper?' asked his uncle.

Gabriel nervously pinched his nose and nodded. 'He said I'd failed in my duty –' he shrugged – 'and then he vanished.'

'Vanished? Just like that?' Sadie raised her hands questioningly. 'Pouff! Into thin air?'

'That's just about it,' Gabriel agreed.

'Well!' Mr Silk sighed. 'Stranger things have happened, I suppose. These are mysterious times.'

'Indeed,' said Hetty.

Mr Silk wasn't quite satisfied. 'Wait,' he said as Hetty turned to go. 'So you're a friend of the cook at Gabriel's school?'

'I'm the assistant cook,' she admitted. 'Sort of apprentice really, learning on the job. I love cooking. And then, because I live in Meldon, Cook recruited me, so to speak.' Hetty began to look nervous. 'This is my first assignment, and I hope I haven't made a mess of it. I've done my best, I'm sure.'

Uncle Jack was still looking puzzled, so Hetty went on to explain that Cook had gathered together a group of people who could be trusted to watch out for vulnerable children. 'Not that Gabriel is at all vulnerable,' she added quickly. 'But because of his great . . . responsibility, I was chosen to watch out for him, and his bag, of course. His designated companion, Albert Blackstaff, appeared to have deserted him.'

Uncle Jack stroked his chin and said, 'I see.' Gabriel noticed that his uncle looked very pale and anxious.

'I think I am what is called a Guardian,' said Hetty, now looking rather flustered.

Sadie suddenly piped up, 'We should look in Gabriel's bag. I mean, it *is* in your bag, isn't it, Gabe? The great responsibility?'

'The cloak, yes.' Gabriel put his bag on the table and unzipped it. Everyone watched as he took out his father's old jacket and unrolled it. There lay the folded cloak, glimmering softly under the kitchen light.

'Wow!' said Sadie. 'All that magic lying on our old table.'

Gabriel grinned. He passed his hand over the velvet and felt – nothing. But it was surely the king's cloak, just as it had been when his father had folded it into the jacket. 'Yes,' he murmured. 'There it is.' But was it? A chill ran down his spine. Something was wrong. He caught Sadie's eye. She looked puzzled.

'Thank goodness,' said Hetty. 'I thought perhaps I hadn't been vigilant enough.'

'All's well, Hetty,' said Mr Silk, looking very relieved, 'and thank you for delivering our Gabriel.'

'It was such an – an exciting experience,' said Hetty beaming, 'but I must dash now. Dad will be freezing. I'll be up at Swallow Farm for a while – so if I'm needed . . .'

'We know where to find you,' said Mr Silk. He saw Hetty to the door and came back holding a black fur hat. 'She gave me this,' he said.

'Albert Blackstaff's hat!' Gabriel exclaimed. 'Hetty put it in her pocket.'

'That man should have told you he was leaving the train,' said his uncle, frowning. 'Your father will have something to say about this.'

Sadie took the hat from her father and hung it in the hall. 'I've cooked your favourite supper,' she told Gabriel when she came back. 'But first I want to show you your room.'

Gabriel laid the cloak carefully in his bag and followed Sadie up the narrow staircase. At the top she led him along a corridor and into the low-ceilinged room he remembered so well. He was unprepared for all the glitter inside, however. Fairy lights hung from the wide oak beams, tinsel decorated the window frames and holly had been slung across the bed's headboard.

'Wow!' said Gabriel.

'It's still Christmas,' Sadie explained.

'It looks great.' Gabriel put his bag on the bed.

Sadie grinned and flicked her long pigtail over her shoulder. 'I'll go and warm up the casserole.'

'Can you wait a minute?' Gabriel drew the cloak out of his bag. 'Something's not right.'

Sadie hovered in the doorway. 'Not right?'

'Sometimes, when I'm feeling a bit down,' said Gabriel, 'I put the cloak on. Dad doesn't mind. And the cloak always changes my mood.'

'Do you feel like the king is there, with you?' Sadie hesitated. 'I know you can sometimes become other people when you put on their clothes. But the king? That would be amazing.'

'Sometimes I see him, but mostly I just feel a great happiness. Not an ordinary happiness, but something very, very powerful.' As he said this Gabriel drew the cloak around his shoulders. 'Oh, Sadie,' he groaned, 'it's gone. There's nothing – nothing.'

Sadie pulled back her pigtail and regarded it with a thoughtful expression, almost as though it were giving her ideas. 'Maybe it was the journey,' she suggested. 'All that shaking about and travelling so far from where the cloak has been living.'

'But I don't feel anything, Sadie. The cloak looks just the same but . . .' he hesitated. 'I can't reach its power. I . . . I can't *sense* anything.'

'Then perhaps it's you,' Sadie suggested.

Gabriel was silent. Not once, since he was four years old, had he ever lost his seventh sense. He had often wished to be free of it, but now, when it was so vital to know what had happened to the cloak, had his seventh sense abandoned him?

'To tell the truth, it does seem a bit – not quite itself, if you know what I mean,' Sadie admitted.

Gabriel nodded dumbly.

'Come and have some supper,' Sadie suggested. 'You'll feel better after you've had some food, and then you can try again.'

'OK,' Gabriel said uneasily. He laid the cloak carefully on his bed

'By the way, if you think Dad's a bit down, it's Cecily, the sorceress. She swooped in on us at dawn this morning.'

'Not the awful stepmother?' said Gabriel, deeply sympathetic. 'And was Septimus the septic mouse with her?'

Sadie nodded. 'And brother dog. Come on, let's forget them.'

Mr Silk had returned to his workroom, but when he smelled cooking he came back into the kitchen. 'Cold weather always makes you extra hungry,' he said.

Sadie's casserole was as delicious as usual, but Gabriel couldn't enjoy it because of a nagging worry about the cloak. Halfway through the meal he decided to try to contact his parents.

'Bad signal here,' said his uncle. 'Try the landline

when you've finished your supper.'

Gabriel bolted down the last chunk of chicken and then phoned his father's mobile. No answer. He tried his aunt's house and one of his cousins picked up the receiver – the youngest, by the sound of it. When Gabriel asked to speak to his mother the little voice chirped, 'Your mum is having a crisis!'

'Crisis?' Gabriel said hoarsely. 'What d'you mean crisis?'

'It's bad,' said the squeaky voice.

Gabriel's stomach lurched. 'I want to speak to my mum, Annie!'

'I'm Alice.' She sounded offended.

'Well, Alice, PLEASE can you get –'

The receiver must have been snatched out of Alice's hand, because, to Gabriel's great relief, his mother said, 'Gabriel, love, are you all right?'

'Yes, yes. I got here, Mum. Why are you having a crisis?'

'Oh, Gabriel, it's dreadful. We've only just heard about poor Albert. They rang us from the hospital. And you went all that way alone.' Mrs Silk spoke very fast, on she went, and Gabriel could only stand there, listening to his mother's jerky sentences in bewilderment. 'Oh, Gabriel, love, are you all right? And the – you-know-what? Dad is so concerned. He's already in Belgium, but he wants to get back as soon as he can.'

Gabriel shook his head and turned a frowning face to Sadie and his uncle.

'Gabe, what's wrong?' Sadie jumped up and came over to him.

Mrs Silk was still rattling on, and Gabriel had to speak over her to say, 'I don't know what you're talking about, Mum. Albert was on the train.'

This brought Mrs Silk to a dramatic halt. Gabriel heard a gasp, then silence. His troubled face brought his uncle to the phone. Taking the receiver from Gabriel, he said, 'What's up, Kate?'

More bubbling chatter from Mrs Silk. Gabriel and Sadie retreated to the table and sat down, but even at a distance Gabriel could hear the hysteria in his mother's voice. At length, his uncle said, 'That's dreadful. A vicious attack, you say? Let us know if anything . . . you know. Yes, Gabriel is quite safe.'

There was another burst of sound from the phone, and Mr Silk said, 'Calm down, Kate. We have the cloak. If this false Albert tried to take it, he didn't succeed. Yes, yes. Goodbye, Kate.

'Bad news,' Mr Silk told the children. 'The real Albert Blackstaff was found in the toilets at Euston Station. Unconscious, his hands tied, in a stall locked from the inside. So you were accompanied by an imposter, Gabriel.'

'He's not going to die, is he, the real Albert?' cried Sadie.

'No, no,' said her father, 'and the cloak is safe, so . . .' He attempted a smile. 'It *is* safe, isn't it, Gabriel?'

Gabriel stared grimly at his uncle. 'No, it's not safe,' he said. He ran up to his room and lifted the cloak into his arms. It looked so familiar, so very like the one he knew, and yet, now, when he held it, the velvet gave him nothing, no warmth, no comfort. This cloak was cold and heavy, as though it had been made by someone without a heart. Holding it as far from his body as he could, he went back to the kitchen. 'It's the wrong one,' he said. 'I knew it.'

'Looks like the cloak I remember,' said his uncle.

'Well, someone has made another one, just like the original. Someone who knew exactly what it looked like.' Gabriel tried not to sound panicky, but he couldn't stop his voice from rising like the whine of an anguished dog. 'The false Albert must have swapped the cloaks while I was getting tea. And then he got off the train.' Gabriel threw the loathsome garment on the floor and sank into a chair.

They all stared at the cloak, twinkling deceptively, even in shadow. Mr Silk picked it up. 'If this isn't the real thing, someone's done an incredible job.'

Gabriel shook his head, and went on shaking it,

until Sadie told him it might fall off.

'I lost it,' Gabriel said dismally. 'The king's cloak. What happens now, Uncle Jack? I mean, you're from the family of Keepers, too.'

Gabriel's uncle looked worried, and it was Sadie who said they would just have to find the cloak, wouldn't they. 'Where did the false Albert leave the train?' she asked.

Gabriel screwed up his eyes, trying to remember. But he hadn't noticed the name of the station, only that it had been the last stop before they got off at Humbledown.

'Hmm,' Sadie said thoughtfully. 'The one before Humbledown is Howgrave. That doesn't help much, I suppose. It's a big town. So he could be anywhere by now.' She glanced at her father. He looked utterly downcast.

CHAPTER FOUR
Into the Hat

'I've got an idea,' said Gabriel. He went into the hall and brought back the false Albert's hat. 'There's just a chance that this could tell us something.' He turned the hat round and round in his hands.

'Gabe, you're a genius!' cried Sadie.

'Not a genius,' Gabriel said solemnly. 'I just happen to have a seventh sense.'

His uncle's eyebrows were knitted with concern. 'Be careful, Gabriel. The head rules the body. A hat could be very dangerous.'

Gabriel continued to turn the hat in his hands. He couldn't deny that he was afraid of it. He'd had some nasty experiences wearing other people's clothes, and he would rather not have to put on this black hat, but there was just a chance that it would show him how to find the cloak. And it had to be found. Before he could change his mind he thrust the hat on to his head.

It was a large hat and slipped down over Gabriel's ears and eyebrows. He blinked uncertainly as the room about him slowly began to disappear. All he could see was a fine white mist. His body was straining under a terrible fear and he seemed to be running in snow. A sharp pain ripped through his back, then another and another.

Gabriel gave an agonised grunt, and fell to the floor. His heart was beating like a drum. It was in his ears and in his head. He was drowning in the sound. It was the only thing in the world. Suddenly he felt very cold. Someone had removed the top of his head.

'Gabriel! Gabriel!' Two voices began to penetrate the thick drumming in his ears. The pounding slowed and faded and he felt a hand on his forehead. Opening his eyes, he looked into Sadie's small, worried face.

'What happened, Gabe?' Her faraway voice came nearer. Behind Sadie, her father, minus spectacles, was holding the black hat.

'I should have stopped you,' said Gabriel's uncle. 'I knew it might be dangerous. How do you feel, Gabriel?'

'OK.' Gabriel rubbed his head and, with Sadie's help, got to his feet. 'A bit unsteady,' he said with a grin, 'but alive. I felt as if I was being shot, or as if what I had become was shot, if you know what I mean.'

'Perhaps you were a bear,' Sadie said helpfully.

'After all, you were in a bearskin hat.'

'That makes sense,' said her father.

'A bear?' Gabriel groped for a chair and sat down heavily. 'Of course, the bear before its skin was a hat. Ugh! That's terrible, for the bear, I mean. I'll try again and maybe I'll get closer to the false Albert.'

'No, Gabriel,' his uncle said firmly. 'It isn't safe.'

Gabriel was secretly glad to see his uncle leave the room with the hat, but he knew he would have to try again. Perhaps, tomorrow, when he felt more awake?

They all went into the cosy sitting room and sat round the log fire. A television flickered in a dark corner, but no one paid it any attention.

The smell of burning pine filled the room. Sadie held chestnuts to the flames with a toasting fork, and Gabriel found his head sinking on to his chest. Warmed right through with hot food and bright, dancing flames, Gabriel was falling asleep. Before he finally lost consciousness he pulled himself to his feet and announced that he was going to bed.

'Sleep well.' His uncle's words came out as though he were hardly aware of them.

Gabriel glanced at him. Uncle Jack was gazing at the fire with troubled eyes, his right hand anxiously rubbing the knuckles of his left.

'I'll come with you,' said Sadie. She kissed her father's head and followed Gabriel up the stairs.

'Goodnight, Sadie!' Gabriel was about to go into his room when he stopped and asked, 'Is your dad OK?'

'No, I told you,' she said sharply. She walked into Gabriel's room and sat on the bed. 'Dad was doing all right,' she said, softening her tone, 'except he couldn't leave the house. I thought that the curse would kind of wear off after a while, like a bruise or something. But a curse is a curse and after three years Cecily still hates Dad.'

'But why?' Gabriel went and sat beside her.

Sadie shrugged. 'She's just cruel. D'you know, she turned a kitten into a toad when she was only three, and she's proud of it. Imagine? And then she turned Septimus's brother into a dog. Her own son. She said it was more peaceful that way, because the boys were always arguing. She's got these awful Fork relatives with big ears. They worship her. They'd do anything she wanted: spy, steal, probably even murder. They came here once, twelve of them. Dad and me stayed in the workshop till they'd gone.'

'I suppose the only person who can lift the curse is Cecily herself,' Gabriel said gravely.

Sadie was silent for a moment. 'Cecily blames my dad for something,' she said, 'but I don't know what it is.'

'Perhaps he knows,' Gabriel suggested.

She gave him a half-smile. 'Dad's very secretive.' With a little wave she walked to the door. 'Night, Gabe.'

Gabriel thought he would sleep well under the welcoming fairy lights, but when he turned off the lights the room became so dark and quiet, he was immediately back on the train, staring into the pale eyes of the hooded stranger. Gabriel shivered and pulled the covers over his head.

Images of the false Albert swam before his closed eyes and, when he tried to banish them, the withered face of the stranger took Albert's place. He must have fallen asleep eventually, because he woke up, very suddenly, as someone left his room. A terrible smell drifted under Gabriel's nose.

He turned on the light and the stars above him began to glow. Leaping out of bed, Gabriel ran to the door and flung it open. 'Who's there?' he called.

Silence.

'Who are you?' cried Gabriel. 'I know you're there. I can smell you.'

Two doors opened almost simultaneously.

'Gabriel?' said his uncle. 'What's wrong?'

While Sadie whispered harshly, 'I can smell him, too.'

The front door banged and Jack ran downstairs. Gabriel followed with Sadie bounding behind him.

Her father flung open the door and they looked out at a stretch of fresh white snow, glistening in the light of the street lamp. Printed deep into the snow a set of large pointed footprints led from the doorstep to the open gate. Jack put a slippered foot on to the step, took a deep, shuddering breath and backed into the hall, clutching his chest.

'Oh, Dad, you forgot,' said Sadie as her father gasped for air.

'Damn that woman!' groaned Jack, sinking on to a chair. 'I only put one foot outside, and it's as if I've been hit by a train.'

Gabriel, heedless of his bare feet, jumped through the snow and stared up the street, and then down to a cluster of trees at the other end. Fresh snow covered the road and the pavement, and there was not one footprint to be seen. Even prowling cats hadn't ventured out on that cold night.

Suddenly aware of his freezing feet, Gabriel leapt back through the snow. 'It must have wings,' he said breathlessly as he hopped inside. 'There's nothing, no footprints, and no one in sight.'

Jack stood up, his legs wobbling. 'That's what comes of ignoring a spell,' he said ruefully.

'A curse, you mean,' said Sadie.' Shall I make some tea?'

'Good idea.' Her father consulted his watch. 'Three

o'clock,' he said. 'I'm not sure we'll sleep with that "thing" hanging about. Let's hope it's gone for good.'

They took coats from the hall stand and, throwing them round their shoulders, padded into the kitchen, which was still warm from the stove.

Noticing Gabriel's snow-wet pyjamas, Sadie suggested he borrow a pair of hers. He wasn't keen but agreed as long as they didn't have flowers on them.

'Birds, if you must know,' Sadie said tersely. 'They were a Christmas present and I haven't worn them, so you won't have any of my nasty experiences.'

Gabriel realised he didn't have much of a choice, his soggy pyjama bottoms were uncomfortable to say the least.

After a mug of tea each, they mounted the stairs, the children already yawning and Jack still shaky but trying not to show it.

When Gabriel had run out of his room he hadn't noticed what lay on the floor beneath the window. Now he saw the pieces of red velvet. Torn, crumpled, muddy strips had been scattered all around his travelling bag.

Gabriel's horrified groan brought Sadie and her father stumbling along the corridor.

'Now what?' asked Jack.

Gabriel pointed to the ruined cloak.

Sadie screamed and covered her mouth. Her father

sucked in his breath and muttered, 'Whatever did that, it's so savage . . .'

An animal, thought Gabriel, unable to go near the mess of torn velvet.

'There's a piece of paper or something under the window.' Sadie approached the ruined cloak. She picked up a scrap of stiff yellow parchment and frowned at it. 'Words,' she said, 'but they make no sense.' She brought the paper to her father who also seemed reluctant to get too close to the mutilated cloak.

Mr Silk regarded the parchment. It was torn at the edges, but not untidily. The writing, in broad black strokes, sloped to the right.

Falfe. falfe. Know this, seven days we give thee, or the cloak will leave thy keeping forever, then 'twill be the worfe for thee.
A Sleepere

'In earlier centuries they would sometimes write an s as an f,' he murmured.

'So, what does it say?' asked Gabriel.

His uncle scratched the back of his head. 'It says, "False, false. Know this, seven days we give thee, or the cloak will leave thy keeping forever, then 'twill be the worse for thee."'

'And the bit at the bottom?' Sadie pointed to the word beside her father's thumb.

'It's signed,' he said, '"a Sleeper".'

'And what does that mean?' begged Gabriel desperately. 'Who are they? Why did they do this horrible thing?'

'It isn't the true cloak,' said his uncle, as if this made the situation any better.

'But why did they do it, Uncle Jack?' Gabriel fretfully tugged at his hair. 'And who? Earlier centuries? But they would be dead by now. It doesn't make sense.'

'It seems that someone is very angry,' his uncle said wearily. 'They wanted to make sure the false cloak was destroyed . . . Let me sleep on it, Gabriel. In fact, we all need our sleep.'

Gabriel looked over at the torn shreds of velvet, and Sadie said, 'Poor Gabe, he can't sleep with this awful thing in his room. I'll get a bin bag.'

'Thanks,' Gabriel said gratefully. He walked hesitantly over to his bed and sat down with his back to the window.

His uncle said good night and told Gabriel not to worry. Nothing was as bad when you looked at it in daylight. Gabriel could hear his uncle stumbling back to his room, muttering to himself, which didn't sound very promising.

Sadie soon appeared with a bin bag and a pair of pyjamas printed with owls. Kneeling on the floor, she gathered every shred of velvet she could see and stuffed it all into the bag. 'Wouldn't it be great if all the bits came together, and when we opened the bag in the morning, the real cloak was there?'

'We'd need a sorceress for that,' said Gabriel, but he gave Sadie a hopeful smile and thanked her for a task that he wasn't brave enough to attempt.

When his cousin had gone Gabriel unpacked his bag, changed into the owl pyjamas and got into bed. For a long time he lay under the comforting lights, reluctant to turn them off.

The next morning they were still twinkling over his head in an encouraging way. Pulling on his socks, Gabriel hurried downstairs. It was still dark but he felt wide awake.

In the kitchen Sadie and her father were already up, eating toast and cornflakes. Sadie tried to smother a grin when she saw Gabriel in the owl pyjamas, but he wasn't bothered about his appearance.

'Have you heard anything about the real Albert?' he asked.

'I've just spoken to your mum –' his uncle cleared his throat – 'and Albert is recovering but he can't remember how he came to be locked in the toilet.'

'Have some cereal!' Sadie pushed the cornflakes

towards Gabriel. He sat down and she passed him a large blue jug of milk.

Gabriel helped himself to cornflakes. He might have been worried, but he was also very hungry. As he gobbled down his breakfast he mumbled, 'I don't want Mum and Dad to know about the cloak. You won't tell them will you, Uncle Jack?'

His uncle brought three mugs of tea to the table and sat down. 'I won't say anything yet, Gabriel. But your father has a right to know. Obviously, the police can't be involved as the cloak is, well, it must remain a secret.'

Gabriel sipped his tea. Sooner or later his father would have to know he'd lost the cloak. Somehow he would have to find it before then. He jumped up and ran into the hall. He returned with the black hat, frowning into it, as though he were searching for a clue. 'If I put it on again . . .' he murmured.

Sadie shook her head. 'You won't get anywhere, Gabe.'

'Perhaps I will. Perhaps I'll get past what happened to the bear.'

His uncle removed his glasses and rubbed his eyes. 'I don't know what to suggest, Gabriel,' he said. 'But you don't have to go into that thing.' He nodded at the hat.

'I *do* have to,' said Gabriel. 'I must find out where

the cloak has gone and get it back.'

'At least put some clothes on first,' Sadie advised. 'You wouldn't want anything awful to happen to you while you were wearing my pyjamas.'

Gabriel had to agree. He dashed upstairs, washed, threw on his clothes and came down, still clutching the hat. 'I'm going to do it now,' he said defiantly. 'I don't care what happens to me.' And with that he jammed the hat on to his head.

He was immediately thrust into the dark. He was falling, falling, ice bit his fingers and stung his eyes; his head was on fire. He dropped to his knees and the darkness became a thin, grey veil. He could see Sadie and his uncle watching him, their faces grave with alarm. Sadie put out her hand and stepped towards him.

'No! No!' Gabriel warned, for now he was entering someone else's life. He had got past his life as a bear, and now he was on a train, and then walking through a town. Next he found himself on a narrow road overhung with trees. It sloped up to a large grey stone building with high round windows and four, no five different entrances. As he drew closer he could see two plain wooden doors, a very tall door decorated with brass bolts and crosses, a black glass door and, at the very end of the building, an arch leading into a shadowy passage.

Gabriel found himself approaching the arch. He entered the long dark passage. There was a metal curtain at the end, he slid it back and on he went, he and the wearer of the hat, who was, presumably, the false Albert. Now they were mounting a flight of stone steps, and suddenly they were in a vast hall with a gleaming slate floor. A huge chandelier hung from the ceiling, holding at least a hundred candles, their flickering light reflected on the swinging spears of glass beneath them.

Gabriel blinked – or was that the false Albert blinking? – for everything was shining; the gleaming furniture, gold-framed mirrors and even the grand piano. And there, in the centre of it all, was a woman in a long black dress with hair like dark steel.

'At last,' she said. 'You took your time.' Her voice was harsh, it grated on the ears like rusty metal.

'Sorry, madam,' mumbled the false Albert.

'The choir will be here any minute.'

'I had to get the disguise right.'

'Everything in place, then?' the steely woman asked.

'Tickety-boo, Madam. Gave the father the wrong time for the train. Made sure he got an invitation to the convention. Even though he's not an alchemist, I was sure he'd accept, being an inquisitive writer. Been watching the friend, he'll probably need the toilet if I can slip something in his coffee. He likes coffee. Cloak sorted. Pretty impressive for a replica, I must say.'

'Of course it is. My spies have studied many depictions of it over the years. Let's get a better look at that disguise then.'

Gabriel felt himself being lifted and squeezed. Now he was folded in half and pushed hard down into the dark. Must be in a pocket, he thought. He uttered a loud moan and then felt his scalp being lifted off. A cool hand touched his face and he looked up into Sadie's wide grey eyes.

'You were making a horrible noise,' she said. She was holding the black, fur hat.

'I wasn't myself,' said Gabriel. He was still feeling a bit shaky.

'Were you him?' asked Sadie, helping Gabriel to his feet.

'The false Albert? Yes.' Gabriel put a hand on top of his head. 'I should have kept the hat on a bit longer. I would have found out more.'

'No, Gabriel.' His uncle pulled out a chair and made Gabriel sit down. 'Sadie did the right thing. You sounded in a bad way.'

Sadie stared eagerly across the table. 'So – what happened?'

Gabriel felt dizzy. He rubbed the top of his head and pushed back his hair. Sadie poured him another cup of tea and he sat looking at it, while Sadie and her father waited, giving him time to collect his thoughts. Images came back to him in quick snatches, but at last he was able to describe his adventure in the fur hat.

Gabriel's uncle frowned. 'The woman you saw, certainly sounds like my ex-wife,' he said.

Sadie looked baffled and chewed her lip. Moments passed and then, suddenly, her father slapped the table and exclaimed, 'Of course, Ludgarth. That's where she is.'

'Ludgarth?' said Gabriel.

'Ludgarth Hall, where her future husband lives.' Jack pulled off his spectacles and grimaced. 'That's the connection.'

'Dad, what are you talking about?' begged Sadie.

Her father began a long description of a city with wide streets and friendly shops, a grand park and a gaily painted bandstand. It was not a town Gabriel recognised from his time in the hat, but then his uncle went on to tell them how the streets narrowed as they led towards the wooded hill behind the city. Standing halfway up, the hall was a tall, slate-grey building with high, round windows, and a steep black roof. A place of sorcery and black magic, built by a family of malevolent magicians. The Loths.

'Have you been there, Dad?' asked Sadie.

Her father nodded. 'Our father took us when we were twelve.'

'You and my dad?' asked Gabriel.

'Yes, it was for a gathering of the Red King's descendants. There were families from all over the world, and then there were people from closer to home. People we knew.'

'Like who?' asked Gabriel.

'Charlie Bone's great-grandfather, James, for one.'

'What about Charlie's uncle, Paton-the-power-booster?' Sadie grinned. 'He's so amazing.'

'No, no. He was only a boy, but he already had this disastrous effect on light bulbs. Poor Paton, they couldn't take him anywhere. But Tancred Thorsson's grandfather was there, thundering about, and Ezekiel Bloor, nosing into everything.'

Gabriel groaned. 'He's a hundred years old and still at Bloor's Academy. His great-grandson can hypnotise people.'

'We had no talents to speak of. But we were Keepers of the king's cloak, and that was enough.' Uncle Jack's expression began to change. 'It's strange, he murmured, 'back then my father always said I was the firstborn, but just before he died he discovered it was Alan. He must have checked our birth certificates, before he passed on the cloak.'

Jack picked up his spectacles and looked at them,

thoughtfully. 'Ichabod Loth was there,' he said. 'He was an odd boy, the same age as us. He had these magnifying glasses that made him look like a fish, and he was always followed by three huge dogs, white with pink eyes. Real monsters. People were terrified of them.'

'Did they bite?' asked Sadie.

'Mm, yes, I think they did. They growled all the time, but it was Ichabod's arms that scared me the most. He could make them grow, literally. They would curl around you from a considerable distance. Ugh! He was also very nosy. He knew our family were the Keepers, but he was curious to know which of us was the oldest. I told him it was me, I always assumed that I was. We're not identical twins, as you know, Alan and me. I'm taller and darker.'

Sadie stared at her father. 'Oh, Dad,' she said slowly, 'you don't think . . .'

Her father frowned, his mouth dropped open, a look of horror passed across his face. He shook his head. 'No, no . . . it can't be.' He took a deep breath. 'I always wondered why Cecily pursued me when your mother died. Cecily enthralled me with a beauty that was false, and a sweet temper that wasn't her true nature at all. I was twice spellbound.'

'She must have known Dr Loth before she married

you,' said Gabriel, 'and he told her you would inherit the cloak.'

'So when Grandpa died, and he left the cloak to Gabriel's dad, not you,' said Sadie, 'Cecily must have been so angry. She threw that curse at you as if it was all your fault.'

Jack sighed. 'She must have wanted it so badly, she was prepared to do anything to get it.' He buried his face in his hands. 'Oh, Sadie, I'm so sorry. It was such a bad time for you.'

Sadie went and hugged her father. 'She has gone and we are happy.'

'I thought she had just come back?' As soon as he said this, Gabriel wished he hadn't because Sadie frowned very hard at him. 'Sorry,' he said.

Gabriel stood up. He was trying to get things straight. It seemed that the awful Cecily had now joined forces with Dr Loth. But who was the hooded man on the train? Nothing to do with the false Albert, or Albert wouldn't have left the train so quickly.

'The man on the train smelled the same as the person who tore the cloak and left that message.'

'The one signed "a Sleeper"?' said Sadie.

'Yes,' Gabriel agreed.

'There might be more than one of them,' she suggested, 'if the letter was signed "a Sleeper".'

'I think I need some air,' said Gabriel.

'The shops will be open by now', said Sadie. 'Let's get the bread. Nice crusty loaves straight from the baker's oven.' She pranced into the passage to get her wellingtons, calling, 'There's a pile of old wellies here. I'm sure I can find a pair to fit you, Gabe.'

'No,' he shouted. 'I mean, I'm sorry, but I can't wear them. Not if they've been worn before.'

'Of course. Sorry.' Sadie returned wearing a pair of pink flowery wellingtons and a yellow mackintosh. 'It must be awful for you. I get all my clothes in second-hand shops.'

'Mine too,' her father ruefully remarked.

'Well, the snow plough's cleared the road,' said Sadie, looking at Gabriel's feet. 'So you can wear your trainers up to the shops.'

Mr Silk followed the children into the hall. He watched Gabriel put on his anorak and Sadie sling a red bag over her shoulder. She opened the front door and walked down the snowy path. Her father stood in the open doorway and said, 'I wish . . .' and he tapped the step with the toe of his shoe.

It was only an inch outside the house, but a curse is a curse. With a gasping intake of breath, Sadie's father staggered back into the hall. 'Damn you, Cecily Fork,' he groaned. 'Let me live!' Clutching his throat, he leaned against the doorframe, struggling for air.

It was the second time Gabriel had seen the effect

of Cecily's awful spell, and he felt increasingly angry. He helped Sadie get her father back into the house, and Sadie made a mug of sugary cocoa. Her father stirred the drink moodily. 'Sorry, you two,' he said. 'It was a silly thing to do.' His voice rose, 'Why doesn't she remove it? What use is it to her, now?'

'She doesn't need a reason,' said Sadie.

Her father gave a grim smile. 'Go on, children.' Jack waved a hand at them. 'We need supplies.'

Sadie was worried about her father, but he insisted that he was fine. So they left him nursing his cocoa and went out.

Gabriel had a lot to think about, but somehow the clear, chilly air and glistening snow made his troubles disappear, for a while. The Christmas trees, sparkling in windows, the twinkling lights, the colour and glitter, all gave him a surge of hope.

The streets were full of merry shoppers, calling to each other over the snow. The stores were all open and the children bought food, wellingtons for Gabriel, and more cocoa. At the top of their road, Sadie cried, 'Race you back,' and off she went down the hill, her long hair swinging from her red woollen hat.

Gabriel had almost caught up with her when the first snowball hit him in the eye. Then came a volley of hard-packed lumps of ice, slamming into his head and his chest. He kept trying to wipe the snow from his face, only to be hit by yet another snowball. A black and white dog made things worse by snapping at his heels.

Sadie was yelling close by, but Gabriel couldn't see her. 'It's the Fork bullies,' she cried. 'Cecily's relatives. I recognise one of them.'

'Why are they . . . doing . . . this?' Gabriel said, gasping as he turned his back on three overweight-looking men.

'Because they like causing trouble,' yelled Sadie.

'But they're grown up,' cried Gabriel.

'So they're worse than children,' Sadie shouted, and she ran at the men, hurling snowballs as she went, but a battery of icy balls slammed into her face and Gabriel's back. There were stones in the snow, Gabriel was sure of it. He staggered forward, trying to keep his balance and protect himself from the next assault.

It never came. Wiping his eyes, Gabriel watched, astonished, as a cloud of snow drove the gang rolling down the road in front of him.

CHAPTER FIVE
A Sinister Message

'Morning, children,' Fred Bean called heartily from his tractor. A large blowing machine, fixed to the front of the engine, was sending jets of powdery snow ahead of it, as fast and furiously as a water cannon.

The children waved while the tractor passed, driving the Fork gang howling down the steep road, and finally into the trees at the end.

Sadie and Gabriel dusted off the wet snow and retrieved the shopping they had dropped, while the tractor turned a corner and disappeared. There was a grinding and a crunching as the big vehicle reversed and then reappeared. Mr Bean had turned off the blower and the tractor came rumbling back up the road.

The children ran to meet it, Sadie crying, 'You saved us.'

Hetty and her father, still laughing, jumped down from the tractor and agreed to come in for a hot drink. They all went into the house and more chairs were pulled up to the table, while coffee and hot chocolate were made. Having little contact with the outside world, Jack was always pleased to see visitors.

While everyone sipped their drinks Sadie and Gabriel took turns in telling their rescuers about the night-time visitor and his sinister message. When Hetty heard what had happened since she last saw the children she was horrified.

'It's much more serious than I had imagined,' she said nervously. 'I'm new to all this and I'm not sure how to proceed.'

Her father gently patted her back. 'You'll manage, my love. You always do.'

Mr Silk looked gloomy. 'We're up against my ex-wife *and* Dr Loth,' he said, 'not to mention a hooded stranger who appears and vanishes at will.'

'Don't you dare lose heart, Jack Silk,' Fred chided. 'We need a bit of optimism here. And I do declare that it's about time you were released from that spell.'

'That'll be the day,' muttered Mr Silk.

Gabriel could see that putting on a brave face was becoming an effort for his uncle. Uncle Jack looked very, very weary.

After a long silence, Hetty suggested that Ludgarth Hall was the only clue they had, and perhaps they should pay it a visit anyway. Hetty didn't seem very positive about this, but Sadie, always keen for an adventure, pounced on the idea.

'Let's go today,' she said eagerly. 'The false Albert probably took the real cloak there last night, and then Cecily rushed off to meet him, once she'd made sure that Gabriel was on the train, coming here with the cloak. We can go in the tractor, can't we?'

Fred Bean chuckled. 'I think you'd better go in the Land Rover,' he said. 'Ludgarth's a bit far for a tractor.'

Not long after Fred and Hetty had gone, there were two phone calls. One was from Gabriel's mother who said that Gabriel was to stay where he was with the cloak for the moment. His father was on the way back from Belgium. He was eager to see his old friend, Albert, and find out exactly what had happened to him.

Gabriel didn't tell her the cloak had been stolen. He didn't want his father to receive too much bad news, all at once.

The other call was from Hetty. The Land Rover had broken down and wouldn't be fixed until tomorrow.

'Huh!' said Sadie impatiently. 'Now we won't get to Ludgarth for another whole day.'

'Perhaps you shouldn't go at all,' said her father.

'Cecily is a dangerous woman.'

'But, Dad, we have to,' Sadie insisted. 'The cloak! What happens if Gabriel can't get it back, ever?'

Gabriel had been wondering why Cecily hadn't used a spell on Sadie. 'Why didn't she bind you to the house, too?' he asked her. 'Or turn you into a toad or something, if she hated you so much?'

'She couldn't,' said Sadie proudly, and from the neck of her sweater, she gently pulled out a thin gold chain. Hanging from the chain was a small, dark green star, its five points tipped with silver.

Gabriel gazed at the star in awe. 'A charm?' he asked.

'It's an obsidian,' Sadie told him. 'My mother gave it to me. It was given to *her* by a white witch called Alice Angel. Mum said it was filled with so much love that as long as I wore it no sorcery could ever touch me. She knew that our family was at risk from such things.' She touched the star with the tip of her finger. 'I sometimes wonder if she guessed what might happen one day.'

Her father gave such a regretful sigh, Sadie quickly slipped the star back under her sweater. 'Cecily does have a problem,' she said, trying to sound cheerful. 'Sorcery tires her out. She was in bed for a whole day after she cast the spell on Dad. It takes a lot of energy to enthral someone that deeply, and when it's spent she can hardly move. And then she can't protect her precious Septimus.'

'That was when the dog nearly got him.' Her father actually smiled at the memory.

'Oh, yes!' Sadie clapped her hands. 'Carver chased Septimus all round the house. Septimus hid in Dad's workshop, crying for his mum, but she couldn't move, and Dad was pretty weak, then, because of the spell. So I opened the workshop door, and the dog rushed in and bit Septimus, so *he* ran outside and stayed there, in the cold, until I took pity on him. I had to catch Carver and tie him to the tree outside.'

'You were a brave girl, Sadie,' her father remarked. 'D'you know, I think that could be one of the reasons why Cecily wants the cloak. It might restore her spent energy, immediately.'

There was almost too much to think about, so after lunch the children decided to make a snowman in the front garden.

Snow began to fall again; such mysterious, soft snow, and it came from a sky that had looked quite clear. As they watched it fall, Sadie said quietly, 'You coming here is the best thing that could have happened, Gabe. The other children in my class are a bit unfriendly. They think I'm odd because Dad is never seen.'

Gabriel said quickly, 'Well, I'm really glad I came, in spite of the cloak – and everything.' He found this was true, because Sadie's cheerful confidence always made him feel better.

The first star had appeared in the sky. The holly on the door glistened in the light from the lamp above it, and the Christmas tree shone in the window. From the outside, The Carpenter's Cabin looked no different from other houses in the street. And yet everyone knew that the man inside was under a spell, and hadn't left his house for more than a year.

Sadie's father had made fruit scones for tea. They were still warm from the oven, and they ate them by the log fire in the sitting room. Gabriel was admiring Sadie's decorations on the tree, when he became aware of a face at the window. At first he thought it was a passer-by, stopping to look at the tree. But when he began to take in the shadowy features, a stab of fear caught in his throat and he stood up, shakily, and pointed at the window.

The others had seen it now. Sadie cried, 'Is that the hooded man?'

Her father strode towards the window and the figure backed away, vanishing into the darkness.

Jack opened the window and put out his head, but instantly he became dizzy. Immobilised by fear, Gabriel stood and stared at the place beside the tree, where the dreadful face had appeared.

Sadie grabbed his arm. 'Shall we go and see?'

Jolted into action, Gabriel rushed to the front door. The freezing air took his breath away, but the sickening smell of decay lingered on the path. There were two footprints under the window. They were made by the same long pointed shoes that he'd seen before. There was also a note, lying in the snow and coloured by the lights from the Christmas tree. The black ink on the parchment was already beginning to run. Gabriel took it inside.

'It's the same paper,' Sadie declared, 'or parchment, I suppose. What does it say?'

The message was shorter than the first, and this time it was not difficult to decipher.

Six days. Get it soon or 'twill be the worfe for thee.
A Sleepere

Gabriel read it aloud, trying not to let his hand shake. 'It's the same kind of writing and it's signed "A Sleepere".'

Sadie took the parchment from Gabriel and stared at it angrily. 'Who is it? Why are they doing this? D'you think the stepmother is behind it, Dad?'

'No,' said her father, drawing the curtains over the

window. 'It has nothing to do with the sorceress.'

'Do you know something, Dad?' asked Sadie. 'Are you keeping secrets from us?'

'No, Sadie, the Sleeper is quite another problem.' Her father settled into his fireside chair again. 'While you were out I called Paton Yewbeam.'

'Paton Yewbeam?' Why wasn't Gabriel surprised? Charlie Bone's uncle Paton was considered to be the most knowledgeable man in the west. He had a vast library of ancient books, some of them containing the stories and legends that surrounded the Red King.

'I don't know why I didn't think of asking him before,' said Mr Silk. 'I asked if there was anything about the king's cloak that a Keeper should know. Anything to do with a Sleeper, for instance; a character from another century, perhaps. Paton said he would look them up in one of his tomes, and ring me back.'

'And did he?' asked Sadie.

'He did,' her father said with a frown. 'But I only heard a few words, and then the line went dead. Another snowfall, probably.'

'Or *him*,' Sadie suggested darkly. 'The Sleeper. Perhaps he doesn't want us to know who he is, or what he can do.'

'What were Mr Yewbeams's few words, Uncle

Jack?' asked Gabriel.

'He said that the Sleepers were mentioned in a book, but . . . And that's when the line went dead.'

'But . . .?' Gabriel rubbed his cold hands together. 'But what?'

His uncle shrugged. 'We'll have to wait. Come to the fire and warm up, Gabriel.'

Gabriel pulled a chair closer to the fire. Sadie put the sinister message on the coffee table and knelt before the flames. All three seemed to have lost the power of speech. Their thoughts meandered in many directions, never settling.

That night, Gabriel knew he wouldn't sleep. How could he? He lay under Sadie's glowing stars, waiting and waiting. For what? His uncle had told him to leave his door open, but how would this help if he had another unwelcome visitor? At last, exhausted by his thoughts, he fell into a troubled sleep.

Next morning, when Gabriel dragged himself down to the kitchen, Sadie greeted him cheerily. 'Well, that was a good night, wasn't it? Nothing happened. No visits, no Sleepers. Perhaps he's gone forever?'

'Perhaps,' Gabriel said dubiously.

'I hope they managed to mend the Land Rover,' said Sadie, as she stuffed her mouth with toast and honey.

Her next words were spluttered through a sticky mouthful and Gabriel could make no sense of them. He could hear his uncle tapping away in his workroom, and couldn't help admiring the way he just got on with things, regardless of Cecily's imprisoning spell.

Several hours passed. The children didn't dare to leave the house. Hetty might arrive while they were out. Sadie tried to ring Swallow Farm, but the line was dead. Finally they decided to walk to the farm instead.

Muffled in scarves and anoraks, with thick socks and boots on their feet, they set off.

It took an hour to reach the farmhouse. Tucked into the side of a hilly field it was barely visible from the road.

Fred Bean was in the yard, working on the Land Rover. He wriggled out from beneath the big vehicle, his face smeared with black oil. 'Nearly done,' he told the children, 'just a few more wheel nuts to tighten and she'll be right as rain.'

'And then we can get going,' said Sadie.

'Not today,' said Fred. 'It's too late. If you want to reach Ludgarth in daylight you need to leave good and early.'

Gabriel was worried. Another day had passed. How many days would be lost before he could even begin to search for the cloak. 'What will he do?'

he muttered.

'What's that, Gabriel?' said Fred, wiping his hands on an oily rag.

'The Sleeper,' Gabriel said uneasily. 'The hooded man. There was another message. It said I had six days to find the cloak, or it would be the worse for me.'

Fred scowled. 'What right does a ruddy hoody have to go frightening kids? Don't you take any notice of it, Gabriel.'

'But Mr Bean, Gabriel can't ignore it,' said Sadie. 'Didn't Hetty explain about the cloak?'

'She told me it was a very valuable, secret thing. I understand all that.' The big farmer's expression suddenly changed. He regarded Gabriel with a kindly sort of understanding. 'There are affairs in this world,' he said gently, 'that I'll never truly comprehend. But when I meet someone like you, Gabriel, well, I get a kind of belief that shakes me up a bit. And I know right well that helping you is, perhaps, the most important thing that I will ever do.'

Gabriel didn't know quite what to say to this. He was very moved by Fred's little speech. Looking at the ground he murmured, 'Thank you, Mr Bean.'

Hetty appeared at the farmhouse door and beckoned the children over. 'Afternoon, children,' she called. 'If you've walked all the way from Meldon, you'll need a bite to eat, and probably a warm-up.'

The children couldn't wait to get into that cosy-looking farmhouse. A delicious smell of cooking had filled the yard as soon as Hetty opened the door.

Once inside, they found that almost every inch of the big kitchen table had been covered with food – cakes of every sort, biscuits, rolls, muffins, tarts, pies, and even a vast plum pudding.

'I just love cooking,' Hetty confessed. 'Help yourselves, children.'

'I don't think we can eat all that,' said Sadie.

'Course not, bless you. I did it for my dad. It'll keep him going for a while.'

'Is your mum still around, Hetty?' asked Gabriel.

Hetty shook her head. 'No. We've been on our own for four years now, me and Dad. Mum died in the same coach as Sadie's mum. It fell into Lake Meldmere.'

'I was six,' said Sadie, absently twisting her hair.

'How did it happen?' Gabriel asked. He had never known how Sadie's mother died. Sadie didn't speak about it.

'The accident?' said Hetty. 'The coach must have swerved on a dangerous bend. It was a narrow road, sixty feet above Lake Meldmere. The passengers were all ladies, a special day out together, travelling round Colley Mountain on the way to the sales in Howgrave.'

Gabriel glanced at Sadie. She was staring out of the window, biting her lip. But he had to ask. 'And it just rolled down the mountain?'

'They didn't stand a chance,' said Hetty. 'Coach just slid down into the lake, one of the deepest.' She shook her head again and dabbed an eye with a tea towel. 'Not a chance.'

'Dad wouldn't talk about it,' murmured Sadie. 'Never, ever.'

Gabriel almost wished he hadn't asked.

'It's all in the past,' Hetty tried to sound cheerful. 'But I miss my mum and expect you miss yours, Sadie.'

'Yes,' Sadie replied. 'Of course I do. Dad does too, and it's worse for him.'

Hetty smiled and then Fred was poking his head round the door and shouting, 'Ta da! All done! She's ready for off, first thing tomorrow morning.'

The children were made to stay at the farmhouse for lunch, and after a hearty meal of roast beef and plum pudding, Hetty drove them home in the mended Land Rover.

'I'll call for you bright and early tomorrow,' she told the children as they jumped out of the car. 'That's a promise.' She was about to drive off, when she suddenly stopped and stared at the front door.

Sadie and Gabriel had already seen it. The lamp

over the front door had been smashed and broken glass covered the doorstep. The Christmas tree stood dark and unlit in the window, yet the room beyond was filled with a soft, flickering light. Fresh snow showed a set of footprints leading to the house – but not returning.

CHAPTER SIX
The Power Booster

'I'm coming in with you.' Hetty swung her legs out of the driver's seat, slammed the door of the Land Rover and strode up the path.

Sadie cautiously opened the door. They all stepped into the house. A smell of burning wax filled the hallway.

Gabriel saw a bulging sack beside the coat-stand and peeped into it. The sack was full of large, white candles.

Hetty looked over Gabriel's shoulder and, in a half-whisper, exclaimed, 'What on earth? Has there been a power cut?' She reached for a switch and the hall light came on, bright in its copper shade.

Jack looked round the kitchen door. 'Turn that light off,' he demanded in an unusually severe tone.

'What's the problem, Mr Silk?' asked Hetty. 'Are you having a fuse problem? I'm pretty good with electrics if you need a hand.'

'*Please*, Miss Bean,' Jack lowered his voice, 'turn that light off or we'll have an accident.'

Hetty switched off the light. 'I'm so sorry,' she said. 'Is it the spell? Are you having a –'

'No,' said Jack impatiently. 'It is *not* the spell. Come and meet our visitor.'

Hetty followed the children into the candlelit kitchen. There they found that the kitchen table had been piled high with exceptionally large books. Their leather bindings looked ancient, some were scratched and ragged, but all were covered in elaborate gold tooling. An interesting smell of old paper and must drifted around them.

The gold lettering glowed softly in the light of an oil-lamp, placed dangerously close to the pile. Gabriel could just make out a few numbers woven between the decorative curls and scrolls, but before he could read the numbers aloud, Hetty suddenly cried, 'Oh, who is that?'

Someone who had been sitting in shadow behind the books began to stand. Up and up and up he came, overtaking everyone else by almost a foot. His longish hair was black streaked with silver, he had grand beak of a nose and his velvet jacket was a rich charcoal grey. Hetty uttered a gasp, and breathed, 'My word.'

Gabriel immediately recognised Paton Yewbeam,

Charlie Bone's uncle. Now the candles made sense. 'Hetty Bean has come to help us, Mr Yewbeam,' he said.

'I know that,' said Paton, 'Cook told me. Sorry to alarm you, Miss Bean. How do you do?' His voice was deep and echoey. 'I thought I'd get here in time to avoid using candles, but dusk always takes me by surprise this time of year. And then there are the Christmas decorations to consider. Luckily, I always travel prepared.'

Noticing that Hetty was still gaping, Paton said, 'I'm a power-booster, Miss Bean. I thought Cook might have told you.'

Hetty shook her head. 'Power-booster?'

'He overloads electric circuits,' Sadie told her. 'All the lights go *boom* when he's near, and then there's broken glass everywhere.'

'Hence the candles,' said Hetty, beginning to understand.

'Hence the candles,' said Paton.

Jack told everyone to sit down while he explained things. When they had all had found chairs, he went on to say that Paton had brought them his invaluable collection of ancient books, because somewhere, in the pile before them, there was a book with a reference to the Sleepers – who they were and why they were following the Keeper of the cloak.

'What I do remember,' Paton patted one of the books and a cloud of dusty fragments flew out, causing everyone to cough. 'What I do remember,' Paton repeated, 'is that the Sleepers were servants of the Red King.' He paused and added, 'From whom all in this room are descended. Except, of course, for you Miss Bean. That is as far as we know, because the king has many millions of descendants.'

'Like Charlemagne,' said Hetty. 'How thrilling.'

Paton bent his head in agreement, and went on, 'Apart from some real gems of little known history, the books tell the story of the Red King's exceptionally long life.'

'Wow, that is a long life,' said Gabriel, attempting to count the books.

'Indeed,' said Paton. 'And I can't remember which volume contains a reference to the Sleepers. My eyes aren't as sharp as they once were, that's why I've brought the books here. I thought if we all took five or six volumes each, we would stand a better chance.'

Sadie and Gabriel exchanged looks. This sounded worse than a whole day of homework. Hetty excused herself, saying that her dad would be wondering what had happened to her. 'But I'd gladly take a couple of books with me,' she said.

Paton seemed almost offended. 'Impossible,' he

said. 'These books are unique, anything could happen to them.'

Hetty looked abashed. 'Sorry,' she muttered. 'Bye, then, all.'

As soon as she had gone they set to work. Gabriel had never stayed up so late, just reading. Paton advised merely scanning the pages. He believed the Sleepers appeared in a chapter with the heading, 'The King's Last Wishes'. But no one could find it.

The flame in the oil-lamp guttered, the candles flickered, and the unfamiliar letter shapes caused the children to squint and rub their eyes. While they read they all snacked on beans and crisps, apples and boiled eggs, and still they felt hungry.

It was after midnight when Jack suggested the children go to bed. They accepted gratefully and climbed the stairs by candlelight. Paton had promised not to visit their rooms and so Gabriel spent another night in the comforting light of Sadie's glowing stars. He was so tired he fell asleep almost immediately, but a loud rattling woke him before dawn.

A cold draught cut across the foot of his bed and he saw that the window had come unlatched. It was banging against the sill. Dragging himself out of bed, Gabriel stumbled across to the window. He was about to close it when something caught his eye. There was a dark form beneath the street lamp on the other side of the road – a hooded figure. It was there for only a second, and then, without seeming to move, it was gone.

'A Sleeper.' It was fear, rather than the biting cold that made Gabriel shiver. He slammed the window, latched it tightly and turned back to the bed. His toe hit something hard. It was a lump of ice, wrapped in maggoty-coloured paper. Gabriel picked it up and rolled back the paper.

Tempus fugit. read the message. It was signed: *A Sleepere.*

Gabriel ran and opened the window. He hurled the block of ice at the lamp post and ran back to bed. All the warm fairy lights in the world couldn't comfort him now. He lay awake until hunger drove him downstairs. Remembering not to turn on any lights, Gabriel felt his way through the dark and into the kitchen.

In one of the candlesticks the stub of a single candle still held a tiny flame. Gabriel could just make out the sleeping forms of his uncle and Paton Yewbeam. Paton's head rested on an open book, Uncle Jack's on the table, the arm of his spectacles caught on his thumb. Both men were breathing heavily. Gabriel tiptoed to the fridge and took out a bottle of milk. He made cocoa, with lots of sugar, but still the two men slept on.

Gabriel sat at the table and peered at the page beneath Paton's head. In the weak light it was impossible to make out any words. Gabriel sipped his warm drink until, feeling safe at last, he fell asleep in the chair.

At sunrise, radiant snow-light filled the large kitchen window, and they all woke up. Sadie stood in the doorway, looking very surprised. 'Did you all sleep here?' she asked.

Gabriel muttered, 'Don't think so.' And then he remembered the Sleeper.

The two men stood up, stretched and shook their heads.

'What brought you down here, young Gabriel?' asked Paton.

Gabriel told them. He ran to fetch the message and showed it to Paton and his uncle. 'What does it mean?' he asked.

'Tempus fugit? It's Latin,' said Paton. 'Time flies. Well, we know that, don't we?'

Jack looked concerned and then Paton said, 'I have some good news,' quickly adding, 'if you can call it that.'

Before explaining anything else, Paton carried the books into the hall, and the two men went upstairs for a 'good wash', while Gabriel helped Sadie to cook a big breakfast of sausages, bacon, eggs, beans, potatoes and thick buttered toast.

Twenty minutes later, they were all enjoying their winter feast, bathed in the brilliant light of the snowy fields outside.

Gabriel was desperate to know what Paton had discovered, but he didn't like to interrupt such concentrated eating. His patience was eventually rewarded when Paton wiped his mouth with a large, white handkerchief and said, 'Now for the Sleepers.'

'Yes?' Gabriel shoved a large forkful of potato into his mouth and stared at Paton.

'The Sleepers,' said Paton, 'are phantoms. That much you will have gathered. They were loyal servants of the Red King.'

'But how . . .' Gabriel began.

Paton lifted a commanding hand. 'Wait,' he said sternly. 'There were three of them; all struck down by a terrible sickness. The king tried every spell he knew to save their lives, in vain. He could take away their pain, but the sickness was unknown to him and too powerful to overcome. Those servants were his favourites and he grieved that they should die so young.'

'Young?' said Gabriel, thinking of the haggard Sleeper.

'Ssh!' hissed Sadie, bouncing in her seat with excitement.

'Young,' Paton repeated. 'Naturally they don't

look so young now, they've led very busy phantom lives for centuries. At least the eldest has.'

Sadie and Gabriel shivered. Jack grimaced and put on his spectacles.

'The dying servants,' went on Paton, 'begged the king that, even in death, they might find a way to serve him. To comfort them he said that, if, in the following centuries, his enchanted cloak was lost or stolen, he would find a way to wake them, so that they could make sure the cloak was returned to the chosen Keepers, meaning, of course, the chosen member of your family, Gabriel.'

'Phew!' Sadie exclaimed, glancing at Gabriel. 'What an amazing history.'

'It seems,' added Paton, 'that the king also granted the Sleepers, as they were called, the power to immobilise anyone that hindered them.'

'But why am I being punished?' Gabriel asked fretfully. 'Why isn't that phantom stalking the thief, instead of leaving me horrible messages?'

'Ah!' Paton went into the hall and returned, carrying another of his books. 'I confess I was puzzled by that too, and then Jack found a vital page concerning Erebus, who could be your phantom Sleeper, Gabriel.'

Pushing plates and cups in all directions, Paton cleared a space and put the book on the table. He opened it to where an impressive red velvet marker had been inserted. 'Here we are,' he said.

'Being so valuable, I imagine the cloak was often stolen,' Jack said quietly.

'Over the centuries, many times,' Paton agreed.

'Lots of awakenings, then,' Sadie remarked.

'Twice or three times every century, for the last five hundred years,' said Paton.

'You'd think the Keepers would take better care of it,' said Gabriel.

Everyone looked at him and he suddenly felt very indignant. 'I was tricked,' he said, but he still couldn't help feeling guilty.

'Let's get back to Erebus.' Paton's long index finger traced a path down the yellowing page. 'The oldest of the three,' he read, 'despairing of successive Keepers' carelessness, decided to make the Keepers responsible for any neglect, and to ensure the cloak was lost forever, if it were not found quickly enough.'

'Seven days, we give thee,' Sadie recited, her eyes very wide. 'Or 'twill be the worse for thee.'

Gabriel could have done without that grim reminder. Dad is the true Keeper, he thought. Why not him? He was glad that his thoughtlessness was not causing his father any harm, and yet . . . 'I'm not the true Keeper,' he muttered.

Paton turned to him, frowning. 'True,' he said,

'but your father, of his own free will, gave the cloak into your protection.'

Gabriel was silent. He stared at the books. 'And there are three of them?' he asked.

'Well . . .' Paton rubbed the back of his neck. 'Only two have been seen. Erebus mostly, Etzel once or twice, but the child, Elissa, has never been seen.'

'Why?' asked Sadie.

'Who can tell? Apparently she brings snow. From what I have so far discovered –' he raised his black eyebrows – 'it seems there has never before been a child Keeper.'

'I'm not exactly a child,' said Gabriel indignantly.

'You might not regard yourself as such,' Paton said drily, 'but you are not yet in your teens.'

Sadie put up her hand, almost as though she was in a classroom. 'Can I ask you just one more thing?'

Paton gave her an approving look. 'Ask away.'

Sadie took a breath and asked, 'Why can't you find anything in all those big ancient books – any spell, or potion or magic to lift a sorceress's curse?'

'D'you think I haven't tried?' said Paton gravely. 'That woman is a powerful force. There is, perhaps, only one thing in the world that can help, and that is the cloak itself.' He closed the book and carried it into the hall. While he was there the doorbell rang and Paton took it upon himself to answer it.

'Oh!' said a surprised female voice, and then Hetty could be heard talking to Paton.

'Children!' Paton called. 'You're off to Ludgarth, now. Not a moment to lose, it seems.'

Sadie and Gabriel quickly flung on their outdoor clothes and ran out to the Land Rover.

'Wait!' called Jack. He held out the black fur hat, and then dropped it, clutching his hand.

'Dad!' cried Sadie, rushing back to his side.

'It was only my hand.' Her father grinned ruefully. 'Take the hat.'

Paton drew Sadie's father back into the hall, while Sadie watched them uncertainly. Gabriel took her hand and picked up the hat.

'I don't think this has anything more to tell me,' he said. 'But you never know.'

Sadie stood motionless. The front door closed and still she wouldn't move.

'D'you want to stay?' Gabriel asked.

She shook her head. 'I'm glad Paton has come,' she said. 'I don't like Dad to be alone for too long.'

They climbed into the back of the Land Rover and found a large hamper on the seat between them. A promise of good things to come.

Hetty looked worried. 'Is your dad going to be all right?' she asked Sadie.

'He's inside now,' said Sadie. 'It was the spell.'

After such a busy night Gabriel fell asleep almost as soon as they set off. It was left to Sadie to describe the events of the night before to Hetty. Now and again a bump in the road, or a snatch of conversation roused Gabriel, but he would gradually nod off again. It wasn't until Sadie gave his shoulder a good shake that he finally yawned and sat up.

The hamper was open. Gabriel saw egg and ham pie, fruit cake, mince pies, cold sausages, crusty rolls, scotch eggs and big lumps of cheese. He sighed with anticipation and took the piece of pie that Sadie offered him.

'There's hot chocolate, too,' said Sadie, holding up a large red flask.

They were parked close to a garage and after a reviving meal, and a visit to the 'facilities', as Hetty put it, they drove on.

Flurries of snow drifted across the windscreen, slowing them down, and the light began to fade.

'I didn't think it would take this long,' said Hetty with a sigh.

The land outside looked bleak and lonely. No houses, no lights and very few trees. And then, at last, a distant sparkle. Hetty put her foot down and soon they were driving into a small town, bright and busy, with an open-air market thronged with chattering people.

They found a car park and jumped out of the Land Rover.

'Now what?' Gabriel turned the hat round and round in his hands. 'This will only tell me about the false Albert when he was wearing it.'

'But he was here before,' Sadie reminded him. 'You saw him when you used your seventh sense. He was in Dr Loth's place, so he'll go back, won't he? Cecily Fork expected him to bring her the cloak.'

'Come on, children.' Hetty tried to sound confident. 'Someone will tell us how to reach Ludgarth Hall, and you might recognise something from your . . . your experience in the hat, Gabriel.'

They walked into the market. Everything was half-price, now that the Christmas shopping was over. Hetty asked a woman selling scarves if she knew Ludgarth Hall.

The woman's face clouded. 'I . . . I . . .' she began.

A group of grim-faced people had suddenly appeared. They wore dark clothes and looked as if they had been to a funeral. They stood at the end of the stall, staring at the woman. They all appeared to have rather large ears.

'I can't say,' faltered the woman.

'But surely . . .' Hetty began. They realised they were going to get no help from the scarf-seller, so they found another stall where a beefy-looking man sold leather goods.

'How much for this?' Hetty held up a red belt.

'Four quid,' the man said cheerfully, and then his face fell.

Gabriel looked over his shoulder and saw the grim-faced group approaching.

'It's the Forks,' Sadie whispered. 'I recognise some of them. Look at their ears.'

'Forks?' said Hetty, 'You mean Cecily's . . .?'

'Relatives.' Sadie screwed up her face and backed away from the stall.

But Hetty wouldn't give up. 'Can you tell us the way to Dr Loth's place?' she asked the stallholder.

'D'you want the belt or not?' snapped the man.

Hetty put the belt back on the stall. 'What's the matter with everyone?' she murmured.

'You're strangers, aren't you?' The man spoke out of the side of his mouth, his eyes on the Forks. 'You'd better get going.'

Gabriel had been watching the group. There were at least ten of them, men and women. They looked deadly serious. And then he saw something else. He held his breath. There was a hooded figure in the distance. Of course, it could have been anyone, but Gabriel wasn't waiting to find out. He took off.

'Gabriel!' cried Sadie, bounding after him.

Hetty turned round. She moved to follow Sadie, but was all at once surrounded by the sinister group. 'Get out of my way!' Hetty demanded.

They stepped closer. Hetty swung her handbag, hitting one in the stomach. The man clutched the bag, pulling it out of her hands.

'I'll call the police,' warned Hetty.

'After you assaulted me?' The man flung Hetty's bag on the ground.

Gabriel kept running. Glancing over his shoulder every few seconds, he dodged round stalls, crept beneath tables, pushed his way through curtains and crashed into boxes. Every time he looked back, the hooded figure was there, a black shadow against the colourful awnings of the market stalls.

Stumbling past a pile of apples, Gabriel tripped and brought them all toppling to the ground. He fell over one, picked himself up, then fell over another. People began to shout at him and a stallholder's dog gave chase, snapping at Gabriel's heels whenever he slowed down. Books went flying, tools, clothing, blankets, pails and hats. A bird cage fell from a shelf and the bird soared out, singing merrily.

Sadie couldn't keep up. She followed the path of destruction as fast as she could. Occasionally she would catch a glimpse of Gabriel's dark head, and then he was off again. A boy seized her swinging pigtail and she yelled.

'What's the hurry, Rapunzel?' he shouted. Sadie swung round and kicked his knee. He let go of her hair and clasped his leg, moaning, 'Little so and so, I'll have yer, so I will!'

'Just try!' shouted Sadie, still running.

Gabriel had reached a wood at the edge of the market. The dog circled him, barking. 'Shut up!' said Gabriel. He picked up a stick and flung it as far as he could. It landed out of sight behind a row of stalls. The dog ran after it, and Gabriel plunged into the trees.

Hot and breathless, he sat in a pile of leaves and leaned back on a broad oak tree. He tried to think but his thoughts whirled. Nothing made sense. Why would no one tell them how to reach Ludgarth Hall? And what would the Sleeper do when he found him? Because the Sleeper *would* find him, Gabriel was quite sure of that.

'And where are the others?' he muttered aloud.

'What others?' said a voice.

Gabriel jumped. He could see no one. Light from the market crept through the wood, causing vague shadows to move against the bare trees.

'What others?' asked the voice again.

'Where are you?' called Gabriel.

A small boy emerged from a clump of bushes. He wore a blue padded jacket and a red woolly hat. 'I'm Tom,' he said, moving closer.

Gabriel stood up. 'Are you alone?' He looked into the trees.

'Very, very alone,' said Tom. He looked to be about seven years old. Gabriel could see tufts of sandy hair sticking out from under his hat.

'I'm Gabriel,' said Gabriel, 'and I'm looking for Dr Loth's place, Ludgarth Hall School. We . . .'

Tom suddenly stopped him. 'The Listeners are on the road,' he whispered.

Voices could be heard. It sounded as if the gang from the market were approaching.

'I don't know why you're here,' Tom said quietly. 'But I don't think you want the sorceress to know, do you?'

Gabriel had to agree. 'We'd better move,' he whispered.

CHAPTER SEVEN
Sadie Alone

Sadie had come to a wooded hill at the end of the market. She called up through the trees, 'Gabriel! Gabe, are you there?'

There was no reply but she could hear several pairs of feet pounding along the track that led up the hill.

'Gabriel?' Sadie called again.

'Ssh!' Someone caught hold of Sadie's hand and yanked her backwards.

'Hey!' cried Sadie.

'Ssh!'

Sadie turned to see three children. A girl of about her age, a boy several inches shorter, and another girl who was very small indeed.

'What's going on?' Sadie demanded.

'Please be quiet,' said the older girl. She had dark, curly hair and wore a bright blue coat. 'You don't want to be caught, do you?'

'Caught?' Sadie questioned. 'What d'you mean?'

'It's not safe to linger near the wood,' said the boy. He looked very like the girl, but wore a tartan jacket. 'We won't hurt you.'

'No, no, no. We won't,' said the little girl, twisting the buttons on her pink anorak. A purple hat with a pink bobble had been pulled over her curls, right down to her eyebrows.

'I'm Lucy Bright,' said the older girl quietly. 'And they're Johnny and Florence,' she indicated the other two. 'Come on, let's get away from here.'

'I'm Sadie, and I'm guessing you're all related.' Sadie found herself walking after the three children. They looked reasonably trustworthy with their rosy complexions and serious faces.

Lucy turned back. 'It's better if you whisper,' she said. 'The Listeners will soon be on the way back to Ludgarth Hall. They have to go up this hill.' She began to run, and the others followed. Sadie brought up the rear.

Leaving the bright lights of the market, they came to a snowy lane running between small cottages and open fields. After several twists and turns, Lucy announced that they were home.

A green gate came into view, almost hidden between two snow-laden hedges. Lucy led the way up to a white front door, and then they were inside a warm house that was decorated with tinsel and holly.

'Mum's working at the market,' said Lucy. 'She'll be back later. We help her in the holidays. You can leave your boots and stuff in the hall.'

The children pulled off their boots and coats and went into the kitchen, where Sadie was given milky tea and fruit cake.

'Can you tell me what's going on?' Sadie asked, swallowing cake as fast as she could. 'I'm really confused. I've lost my cousin and the person that brought us here. We came looking for Ludgarth Hall. Someone stole something very precious that belongs to my cousin, and we think the thief has taken it to the hall.'

The Bright children all looked very anxious.

'You can't go up there,' said Lucy. 'Our neighbours, three sisters, well, they went up there, and they never came back. Tom, their little brother, has been waiting and waiting for them. He was all alone on Christmas day, but we didn't know then. Mum makes him come and sleep here, but every day he goes off again, to wait on the hill. It's very dangerous up there, in Ludgarth Hall School.'

Sadie took a breath. 'I know it's a bit risky –' she began.

'You mustn't!' Johnny leaned across the table and stared into Sadie's face. 'The sorceress is there. She

103

brought the Listeners and she's doing things to people.'

Sadie hesitated, and then she said, 'I know all about the sorceress. She was my stepmother for a bit, and I've met her relatives. They're all villains.'

The three Brights gasped and Lucy shook her head, several times, saying, 'How could your dad have married a sorceress?'

Sadie couldn't think how to explain, but a small voice at the end of the table, said, 'She put him under a spell, didn't she? Like the Snow Queen did to Kay in the story.'

'Yes, Florence,' Sadie agreed. 'It was just like that. He couldn't see how cruel she was until she left him, and then she put him under an even worse spell. My poor father can never, ever leave his house, not for one second.'

'But why did she enthral him in the first place?' asked Lucy.

Sadie could see that she would have to tell the Brights more than she had wanted. Lucy was obviously someone who liked to have all the facts.

'We think it was because of something secret and magical,' said Sadie. 'An ancient king left this thing to our family – in perpetuity.'

'That means for ever and ever,' Lucy explained to her siblings.

Sadie nodded. 'The sorceress wanted this thing

desperately, and she thought my father would inherit it, but it went to my uncle instead.'

'She must have been consumed with rage,' said Johnny dramatically.

Sadie agreed. 'But we think the sorceress might have got the precious thing now, because my cousin, Gabriel, lost it on the train. I can't explain it all, but we think it might have been taken to Ludgarth Hall.' Sadie then had to describe the phantom Sleeper who was tormenting her cousin.

The three Brights stared at Sadie, their eyes wide, and their mouths open in silent gasps.

'Anyway –' Sadie stood up and squared her shoulders – 'I'd better go on looking for Gabriel, and Hetty who brought us here.' She thanked the Brights for tea and went to fetch her coat.

The three children followed Sadie into the hall, and Lucy gave her a torch, telling her to keep to the shadows.

'Ludgarth Hall is on the hill where we found you,' said Lucy, 'but I wish you didn't have to go there. Come back to us if you don't find your friends.'

'Definitely,' said Sadie. Her need to find Gabriel was calling her away, but it was with some reluctance that she left the Brights with their friendly faces and cosy home. As she set off down the snow-filled lane dark clouds drifted across a dangerous-looking green sky.

Sadie began to run. When the market lights came into view she moved closer to the hedges. She remembered the Forks surrounding Hetty. What had happened to her?

Sadie came to a halt. The hill of shadowy trees loomed before her. And there was the lane that must lead to Ludgarth Hall.

'I can't go up there,' she told herself, pinching her hand to give herself courage. 'Not alone, anyway.'

'Sadie!' came a harsh whisper.

'Wh . . . who?' Sadie asked in a small voice.

'You sound like an owl.' Gabriel emerged from the trees, followed by a small boy in a red hat.

Sadie was so relieved to see her cousin she uttered a cry of joy and flung her arms around his neck. 'I thought, I thought . . . I don't know what I thought,' she mumbled into his shoulder.

Gabriel gently removed her arms. 'I'm OK,' he said. 'Although not everything is OK. This is Tom.'

'Hi!' Sadie peered at Tom in the deepening gloom.

The small boy gave a nervous smile.

'Tom lost his sisters,' said Gabriel. 'Up at the Hall.'

'Oh, you must be the Brights' neighbour,' said Sadie. 'They gave me tea.'

'They're friends,' said Tom.

'Let's get going,' Gabriel said impatiently. 'I want to get into that place before dark.'

'It *is* dark,' said Sadie. 'And what about Hetty?'

'And the Listeners,' said Tom.

Gabriel pushed the hair out of his eyes. 'I don't know what to do now. It could take ages to find Hetty. And surely we can avoid the Listeners if we're careful.'

'We must find Hetty,' Sadie insisted. 'She'll be frantic.'

Gabriel gave a huge sigh. 'But the Sleeper,' he moaned. 'What will he do, if I don't . . .' His words tailed off into a gasp and he stared down the lane, his eyes so wide, Sadie thought they might drop out of his head.

Approaching slowly in a curious floating manner was a hooded figure. The glimmering air about it swam with small winged insects. They did not fly, but drifted rather, in the unnatural light. On both sides of the figure, the snowy verges had an odd green shimmer, and the air was thick with the scent of mould and spices.

'Run!' cried Sadie, grabbing Gabriel's arm.

Her cousin was transfixed. He seemed unable to move.

Hetty Bean had found her way to the local police station. She was now sitting on a hard seat beside the door. The police didn't appear to be the least bit interested in her predicament, but she refused to leave.

'Where am I supposed to go?' she had asked the desk sergeant. 'I've searched the market for those children, but they've vanished. They were in my care, I'm responsible. Can't you do something?'

'We're a bit stretched this time of year,' said the sergeant. 'Someone'll find 'em, and they'll turn up right as rain.'

And that was that.

Hetty wished Cook hadn't sent her on this mission. She'd just returned from visiting her father for Christmas, and the very next day Cook had rung up and told her to pack a bag and go back to the train station.

'No buts, Hetty,' Cook had said. 'There's not a moment to lose.'

'But . . .' Hetty couldn't help that last 'but'.

'I'm relying on you, Hetty. You know some of the children in this school are, well, different. They're special, and we need to keep them safe.'

'I'm not a childminder,' Hetty had protested.

'No one is suggesting that,' Cook had said in a cross voice. 'But your father lives near Meldon, doesn't he? And I've just heard that Gabriel Silk, you know, the lanky boy with the seventh sense, well, he's off to Meldon with something precious – a cloak of inestimable value. He'll be alone, except for some unknown friend of his father's. I want you to watch them, Hetty. I NEED you to watch them.'

'I don't think –' Hetty began nervously.

Cook wouldn't allow her to say another word. 'I'm enrolling you in our network, Hetty,' she went on. 'You shall be a Guardian. A great privilege. Consider this the first of many assignments. The train for Meldon leaves here at two-thirty.'

'Oh?'

'And Hetty, I shall have to swear you to secrecy. You must promise never to reveal this venture and the reason for it, to anyone. Although, of course, your father may be permitted some knowledge of it. Do I have your promise?'

'I promise,' said Hetty, swept along by the drama of it all.

Cook had put down the phone and Hetty had been left with no options.

An hour passed. Gabriel and Sadie had not turned up. Hetty was feeling tearful. She could hear people leaving the market. It was dark, and very cold.

A woman marched into the police station. The doors banged shut behind her. She wore a thick brown coat and a white woolly hat with a bobble on the top. Her boots were rimmed with snow.

The desk sergeant looked up. 'Not you again, Mrs Bright,' he said irritably.

'I told you,' said the woman, striding up to the desk, 'I shall be in here every day until you find those girls.'

'And I've told you, I don't know how many times, that they're spending a few days in the hall, at Dr Loth's invitation.'

'But what about the boy?' Mrs Bright was almost shouting. 'He's all alone. Only seven years old. Those girls would never have left their little brother alone at Christmas, especially with their parents visiting a sick granny on the other side of the world.'

'Well they DID,' said the sergeant. 'Speak to Social Services.'

'I HAVE!' cried Mrs Bright, banging the desk with a gloved fist.

'TRY AGAIN!' the sergeant shouted back in her face.

What a horrible, unhelpful policeman, thought Hetty. She was feeling increasingly helpless herself, but also intrigued.

Mrs Bright stamped her foot and strode back to the door. She was about to open it when Hetty jumped up and ran towards her. 'Excuse me,' she said, 'but you mentioned Ludgarth Hall.'

'I did,' said Mrs Bright.

'Well, it's funny you should say that, but –'

'Let's go outside,' said Mrs Bright.

Hetty followed the woman out on to the street.

'They're hopeless in there,' said Mrs Bright. 'Something has to be done about them, and soon.'

'Ludgarth Hall?' Hetty reminded her. 'You know where it is?'

'Everyone does,' said Mrs Bright. 'Although it's not easy to reach, and at times impossible to enter.'

'Oh, no,' moaned Hetty.

'What is it, dear?' the woman had kind eyes and a friendly smile. 'Why d'you want to know about the hall?'

'There are some children in my care; I think they might have gone there.'

'Why on earth would they do that?' asked Mrs Bright, looking concerned. 'I know it's a school – of sorts – but the children are all on holiday – except for those poor Touchstone girls. Perhaps your charges are carol singers?'

'No, no . . . they, they . . .' Hetty stammered, wringing her hands.

'Whatever is it, please tell me. You look done in.' Mrs Bright touched Hetty's clasped hands.

The kindness was too much for Hetty, her eyes filled with tears and she poured out her troubles. Without mentioning the cloak, she told Mrs Bright everything that had happened, from the moment Cook enlisted her as a Guardian, until she had reached the police station. As she rattled on, she wondered what had come over her. She never usually behaved like this with complete strangers. But she had no one else to turn to, and from what she had heard in the police station, Mrs Bright had a similar problem.

Mrs Bright didn't flinch at the mention of a hooded spectre, or even a wicked stepmother, and a boy with a seventh sense. 'You poor dear,' she exclaimed, clutching Hetty's shoulder.

'Hetty,' said Hetty, a bit tearfully. 'I'm Hetty Bean.'

'And I'm Mary Bright.'

They smiled at each other and shook hands. Hetty immediately felt better. Mary Bright insisted that Hetty should come home with her, and they would try to decide what to do next.

As they walked along the snowy lane together, Mary told Hetty all about the troubles that had suddenly descended on Ludgarth. 'The police are not doing their duty, Social Services won't help deserted children, and the council seem to be completely oblivious to everything that is happening. It all started when that woman arrived. Quite frankly she appears to have bewitched everyone.'

'What woman?' asked Hetty, although she already had a pretty good idea.

'She calls herself Cecily Fork. She's very tall, hair like a steel helmet. She's frightened them all. I don't know how, but she seems to have a way of getting exactly what she wants. People are calling her a sorceress.'

'The sorceress.' Hetty grimaced. 'The stepmother. It's the same woman. She laid a curse on someone I know. If she's here, no wonder everything has gone wrong. I think I met her relatives in the market. Grim faces, big ears.'

'Yes, I believe the Listeners are all related to her,' said Mary Bright. 'And now she's got herself engaged to Dr Loth. He's a dreadful man. With the pair of them in charge, I dread to think what'll become of us all.'

When they got to Mary Bright's house, a situation that had seemed bad enough suddenly became much worse.

Mary took Hetty into the kitchen, where they found Johnny and Florence sitting close to the stove. They looked anxious.

'Is Lucy in her room?' asked their mother.

'No, Mum, she's gone to the hall,' said Johnny.

'The HALL?' cried his mother. 'Alone?'

'I wanted to go with her,' Johnny said defensively, 'but she said I must stay with Florence.'

'How long has she been gone?' asked Mary.

Johnny looked at the clock on the mantelpiece and frowned.

Florence said, 'Ages and ages.'

CHAPTER EIGHT
The Green Phantom

Gabriel was still standing motionless on the road.

'Gabriel!' hissed Sadie, grabbing his hand. She tried to pull him back, but he couldn't or wouldn't move. The hooded figure seemed to have a magnetism that held Gabriel in its grip.

On it came, hovering, drifting, the soft light around it brightening every second.

'What is it?' Tom clutched Sadie's other hand.

'A phantom,' she whispered.

'A phantom is a ghost,' Tom said in a hushed voice. 'But this thing isn't . . . I can smell him. It's the smell of something very, very old.'

'He *is* old,' Sadie told him. She gave Gabriel's hand another tug and pleaded, 'Gabe! Move, *please!*'

Gabriel said quietly, 'It isn't the same one.'

Sadie peered at the hooded face. This phantom was not old and decayed. From what Sadie could see of him beneath the hood, he was a young man. He looked a little worn, and the bones of his face showed clearly beneath the milky-grey skin, but his bright eyes twinkled out of their withered sockets, and he was smiling.

'I don't think he means us any harm,' said Gabriel.

At that moment the stranger lifted a hand, his palm towards then. 'Etzel!' he said, in a light, slightly hollow voice. 'Greetings, Keeper!'

Gabriel found himself copying the young man. 'Greetings,' he said, lifting his hand.

'Etzel,' said the phantom.

'What does that mean?' Gabriel murmured.

Sadie remembered the names in Paton's book. She nudged Gabriel. 'Etzel is his name.'

'Of course. I thought it was a foreign word.' Gabriel cleared his throat and said, 'Etzel', and then, pointing to himself, he said, 'Gabriel.'

Tom leaned close to Sadie and whispered, 'What's going on?'

Sadie gave his hand a reassuring squeeze. 'We'll tell you later.'

The hooded phantom now stood before them, and the spicy, musty smell was so overpowering that one by one the children sneezed.

''Tis as I feared,' said Etzel. 'Time doth alter a perfume once so pleasing.'

Sadie was delighted. 'You really do talk like

116

someone from the past,' she said.

Etzel smiled. His teeth looked very good, considering their age. 'Keeper Gabriel, we have work,' he said, staring at Gabriel with his bright twinkling eyes. 'The cloak – but first a thief.' He turned around, and looking up at the sky, said, 'I am here, oh King, to aid the young Keeper.'

The children watched the young man turn and turn, smiling into the heavens. His hood fell back, revealing a head of thick brown curls and beneath the flying folds of his long grey shroud, they could see a green velvet tunic embroidered with golden flowers. A wide jewelled belt encircled his waist and his stick-thin legs were clad in wrinkled green stockings. On his feet he wore green and gold shoes with exceptionally long, pointed toes.

Sadie, lost in admiration, breathed, 'What very fine clothes.'

Etzel came to rest. 'I thank thee.' He bowed.

'Oh!' said Sadie, impressed by the bow. 'You're welcome.'

'So where art thou bound, Keeper?' asked the phantom.

'Up to Ludgarth Hall,' said Gabriel nodding at the hill. 'I think the cloak might be there.'

'For thou hast the seventh sense,' said Etzel.

'I hath,' Gabriel agreed.

Tom nudged Sadie and whispered, 'Why is Gabriel talking funny?'

'He's being polite,' she told him.

Etzel cupped his ear and grinned. 'My speech is strange to thine ear, youngest one, yet for me thy words have a curious ring to them.' He gave a giggle.

Bewildered by the phantom's speech, Tom shrugged and rolled his eyes.

'Come, then, to the Hall of Ludgarth.' Etzel whirled around and began to move up the lane in his odd, drifting motion.

The three children followed, Tom still clinging to Sadie's hand, while Gabriel walked ahead, a footstep away from the dusty glimmer that accompanied the phantom.

'My aura will not harm thee,' Etzel said.

'Then I'll . . .' Gabriel moved to Etzel's side and they walked together up the lane.

Gabriel found it surprisingly pleasant to be surrounded by softly floating insects. Now and again they would tickle his face or tap gently on his head. And the greenish glimmer made it easier to see the ruts and loose stones that littered the lane.

'So, um, you, that is thou,' Gabriel began, not quite knowing the correct way to speak to the phantom, 'thou wast a favourite of the Red King?'

Etzel turned a smiling face to Gabriel and nodded.

'I died,' he said, 'yet went happily to my rest, for my phantom could yet serve my king.'

'But why three phantoms?' asked Gabriel.

'One to lead, one to accompany, and one to . . .' Etzel gave a choked cry, bent his head and covered his face with his hands.

The little group came to a standstill. They surrounded Etzel whose loud sobs echoed down the lane.

'Is it . . . is it something to do with the third . . . um . . . phantom?' asked Gabriel.

'My sister,' Etzel wept, wiping his eyes with his knuckles. 'The sweetest soul and of such tender years. She languished in a bitter winter, and yet she rejoiced in snow. I passed a sickness to her – cursed Etzel – the blame is all mine.'

'Oh, I'm sure it's not.' Sadie gave the phantom's arm a comforting pat and found it reassuringly solid. 'I believe those old sicknesses affected everyone,' she went on. 'No one could escape them. Whole villages were . . .'

'Sadie!' hissed Gabriel. 'Don't go on about sickness.'

'Sorry,' Sadie muttered.

But it seemed to have done the trick. Etzel lifted his head and smiled at them. 'Thou speakest true, Say-dee,' he said. 'Onward then.'

He drifted up the hill again, and the children had to run to catch up with him. Now the lane began to bend round an outcrop of rock, and then again round a clump of trees. As he ran, Gabriel asked Etzel why the phantom on the train had tormented him so horribly, and why he looked so very, very old.

'Erebus was a man of little patience,' said Etzel. 'He hath so oft been harried from his tomb by careless Keepers ever losing that precious cloak, he tried another tack. He would not lead, but drive those slip-shod, thoughtless Keepers to their duty.'

'And, perhaps, if he was above ground so many times, he aged faster than you did?' Sadie suggested.

'A lot faster,' said Gabriel.

'Just so,' Etzel agreed.

'But I wasn't careless,' Gabriel complained. 'I left the cloak with someone I thought my father trusted, just for a few minutes, and – wham! – there was Erebus, even before the awful imposter had left the train.'

'Train . . .?' Etzel looked bewildered.

'Oh, a sort of carriage,' said Gabriel, thinking of the nearest thing to a train that Etzel might understand.

'Don't forget,' Sadie reminded Gabriel, 'the thief had already swapped the cloaks when Erebus appeared.'

Etzel sighed. 'We were called,' he said 'for the cloak

was taken. We had no choice but to appear. I am heartily glad, however, to meet such genial strangers.'

Sadie smiled. 'I thank thee,' she said.

All at once, Tom piped up, 'But when will your sister come? And what's she supposed to do?'

Etzel lifted his head and seemed to consult the heavens. After a long silence that none of the children dared to break, he gave a long sigh and said, 'Elissa was to answer. 'Tis my belief that she only wakes when all is almost lost, for only once hath she answered, long, long ago, in a storm of snow. In the centuries since, she sleepeth still.'

Sadie said thoughtfully, 'So only one person has ever called to her –'

She was interrupted by a blood-curdling shriek from the lane behind them.

Etzel was the first to move. He sped down the lane as though he were flying. In fact, perhaps he was flying. His grey cloak sailed behind him like a single great wing.

'Who art thou?' Etzel called in his singing, hollow voice.

The children ran after him – Gabriel, Sadie and then Tom, panting, 'Wait for me!' They rounded the bend and gathered behind Etzel who had spread his arms.

Beyond the phantom three huge white dogs stood

with their backs to Etzel. They were emitting low, terrifying snarls as they advanced on someone cowering in front of them.

Sadie shone her torch at the small figure and recognised her. 'Lucy!' she cried.

Lucy Bright had fallen to her knees. She was shaking with fear. 'Help me, please,' she moaned. 'They're Dr Loth's dogs, and they'll kill me.'

The great dogs were almost upon her. Crouching like lions, their snarling increased in depth and savagery as they approached the petrified Lucy.

Suddenly, another sound tore through the air. Was it a whistle, a cry? No one could be sure. The children had never heard anything so piercing and unearthly. They realised that it could only have come from Etzel.

'Be still, unworthy curs!' he commanded.

The white dogs stiffened. They hunched their massive shoulders, raised themselves a little and turned to face Etzel. At the sight of him they shivered violently, lowered their heads and whined in terror. The next moment they were lying on the ground, their eyes glazed and their great jaws hanging open in silent howls. Gabriel thought of Hetty on the train, frozen before Erebus.

Etzel beckoned Lucy, but she wouldn't move. The dogs might be motionless but she was still afraid.

The phantom and his glimmering green light was no help at all.

'It's OK, Lucy,' called Sadie, 'our friend, the man who frightened the dogs, he's just a . . . a . . .'

'A friendly phantom,' said Tom.

This wasn't much help to Lucy either. 'A phantom?' she squeaked.

Gabriel decided to make a move, but first he had to make sure the dogs were out of action. 'Are the dogs going to move again?' he asked Etzel.

'They will not stir,' said the phantom. 'I have used the power the king invested in me, to drain the creatures of life and strength, just for a while.'

'When will they – get their life and strength back?' asked Tom.

Etzel merely shrugged, so Gabriel decided to take a chance. He ran carefully past the lifeless dogs and down to Lucy. 'I'm Gabriel,' he said. 'Come on, Lucy. You'll be OK. Etzel's here to help us.'

Lucy gave him her hand, and together they ran round the prone white bodies, and up to the others.

'I was worried about you,' cried Lucy, hugging Sadie. 'So I came looking for you, and then those beasts cornered me. I tried to hide from them, but they sniffed me out.'

'You're safe now,' Sadie told her.

Etzel smiled in agreement. 'To the hall,' he urged, 'before the glass is drained.'

This sounded a bit worrying, but they all trotted after the phantom. There was really no alternative.

'Why is he here?' whispered Lucy as they plodded up the lane. 'And where does he come from?'

'I'm not quite sure,' Sadie replied softly. 'But he's come to help Gabriel.'

They walked round another bend and there it was: a towering mansion stood at the end of the lane. It was now quite dark, but an avenue of bright lamps led to the door, and they could see the high round windows, and massive grey stones of the building.

The sight of Ludgarth Hall, now that they were actually close to it, brought them all to a sudden halt. Was it really necessary to approach that grim place? Did they have to go into an unknown building, where a sorceress lurked?

The imposing sign on an iron post at the beginning of the avenue of lamps did nothing to reassure them. It said:

Ludgarth Hall: School for the Darker Arts
Principal: Dr Ichabod Loth

'I've never been in there,' Tom said uncertainly, 'but I know it's a school for children with . . . um . . . special abilities. They even sleep there during term-time.'

Lucy added darkly, 'Only children who want to improve their so-called magical skills. Children like us aren't allowed.'

'But carol singers from the village can go in at Christmas,' Tom reminded her. 'The choirmaster, Mr Puzzle, is really friendly. He comes to the village sometimes.'

Gabriel squared his shoulders. 'Well, we're here now, so we'd better try to get in.'

Sadie said quickly, 'And out again.'

''Tis the place, then,' said Etzel. 'I must bid thee farewell.'

'WHAT?' cried the children.

'You can't leave us now,' said Gabriel.

'I will be with thee, by and by,' said Etzel, with a smile, and with that he vanished.

'Trickster!' called Gabriel into the empty air. 'Where have you gone? You brought us here. You're supposed to help me.'

Sadie tugged his sleeve. 'That wasn't the deal, Gabe. Remember, he was only supposed to *accompany* you. He didn't say he had to help us.'

'But he's *not* accompanying us,' said Tom. 'He's gone.'

'Perhaps we'd all better go home,' said Lucy.

'No!' said Gabriel. 'I must find the cloak.'

Tom wailed, 'My sisters! I've got to find them.'

'Sorry.' Lucy looked embarrassed. She and Sadie exchanged glances, and Sadie said, 'I think we'd all better stick together.'

So all four squared their shoulders and walked together down the long avenue of lamps. On both sides parked cars could be seen, their windows winking in the lamplight. You could hardly miss Cecily Fork's massive vehicle.

'She's here,' Sadie whispered.

Gabriel said, 'I suppose we expected that.'

They pressed on and didn't stop until they reached the great oak door. It was studded with shiny brass bolts and crosses, but there was no bell. Instead a brass knocker, shaped like a giant beak, hung in the centre.

'There are five doors,' Tom whispered. 'If we go in this one we'll come to the great hall. My sisters went in there, for carol singing. I came with them, but I wasn't allowed in.'

'So that's no good,' said Gabriel, 'and the archway leads up to a huge room where I met the sorceress – well, where the false Albert met her.'

'You've been here before?' asked Lucy in surprise.

'Sort of,' Gabriel confessed.

Sadie added, 'We'll explain later.'

'HEY!' said a voice, somewhere near their feet.

Gabriel leapt round and the same voice said,

'Watch it, young man. You'll squash me.'

They looked down at the paving stones beneath their feet, and Sadie trained her torch on a small creature.

'It's a weasel!' she squeaked.

It certainly looked like a weasel. Larger than a rat, but smaller than a stoat, it had reddish brown fur, a white chest, long white whiskers and bright button eyes. It was standing on its hind legs.

'Sorry to alarm you,' said the weasel. 'I don't usually look like this.'

'You sound like Mr Puzzle, the choirmaster.' Tom was peering closely at the weasel. '*Are* you Mr Puzzle?'

'I was,' said the weasel, 'but *she* caught me out.'

'The sorceress?' asked Gabriel.

The weasel uttered a scornful 'Huh!' and then said, 'You'd better follow me. This is a dangerous spot. Her spies are always lurking behind it.' He sped away in long, leaping bounds. The children had to run to keep him in sight, but he eventually stopped beside a small door of plain, polished wood.

'This is the servants' entrance,' said the weasel, panting. 'Whew! I'm not used to running so fast with such short legs.'

'Mr Puzzle,' said Tom, 'I'm Tom Touchstone. Do you know what happened to my sisters?'

The weasel sighed. 'I imagined you were looking for those poor girls,' he said.

'*Please*, what happened to them?' begged Tom. 'They just came up here for carol singing, and they never came back, but you must have seen them.'

'I believe I know where they are, but . . .' The weasel's head drooped. He scratched his stomach while everyone waited for him to continue. 'But they are much changed.'

'They're not weasels, are they?' cried Tom.

'No, no, they look the same as they did,' Mr Puzzle assured him. He turned to Gabriel, 'You, boy.'

'Gabriel Silk,' said Gabriel. 'And this is Sadie, and that's Lucy.'

'Yes, yes,' said the weasel impatiently. 'Gabriel, turn that door handle, will you? I can't reach it, and we mustn't be caught here.'

'Why did the sorceress do this to you, Mr Puzzle?' Tom asked anxiously.

'Long story,' muttered the weasel. 'Turn that handle, boy!'

Gabriel turned the brass doorknob and was surprised to find the door swung open with hardly a sound.

The weasel leapt into the house and the children quickly followed. Gabriel, the last one in, carefully closed the door behind him.

They were now in a long well-lit passage with several doors leading off it. One was open and they glimpsed shelves of tins and jars, before the weasel hurried them on. As they approached the door at the end, a burst of hearty singing could be heard. It seemed to be in a foreign language.

'The school cook, Luigi, is my friend,' the weasel explained. 'He's Italian. Very nice. Very good food.'

Gabriel wished the weasel hadn't mentioned food. He was made all the more aware of his own hunger. His stomach had been rumbling for quite some time.

'You'll have to open the kitchen door,' the weasel advised. 'I've been having to wait for one of the staff to open it, and they often knock me over.'

When they reached the door, Gabriel looked in through the glass panel at the top. Everyone in the kitchen was busy. There were at least six people besides the enormous chef. He was stirring something in a large pan on the counter. Behind him a blackened stove ran almost the entire length of the vast kitchen.

'Come on, open up,' said the weasel.

'But they're going to see us,' said Gabriel.

'What if they tell?' asked Lucy.

'Oh, goodness, they won't tell,' said the weasel. 'None of them speak English. Two are from a part of Africa where they only speak French, three are from

Italy and two are Mongolian. Luckily I am familiar with all three languages.'

The children were impressed, but Sadie couldn't stop herself from asking, 'And can you speak weasel?'

Mr Puzzle obviously didn't think this worthy of an answer. He told them that all the staff were his friends, because he understood them and had helped them to overcome the many problems they encountered while working in such a difficult and dangerous house. 'I trust them completely,' he said. 'They are naturally worried about your sisters, Tom, but they are so frightened of the sorceress, they dare not do anything to anger her. They are also very sympathetic to my new . . . situation, and do their best to meet my needs.'

Tom said, 'I expect they are a very different sort of needs now.'

'Not so different,' said the weasel. 'I still enjoy spaghetti bolognaise. Now open this door, we can't stay here all day.'

Gabriel hesitated. Could they trust the weasel? After all, weasels didn't have very good reputations.

'Come on!' Mr Puzzle demanded, stamping his back foot. 'I am NOT a weasel, if that's what you're worried about. *She* did this to me because she found out that I had advised Ichabod Loth not to marry her. "You weasel," she screamed, pointing her long,

long finger at me. And that was it. I found myself furring up, whiskering, shrinking, but I scarpered before she could take my voice away.' He waved a paw. 'Oh, never mind all that. Just open the door.'

'Sorry, Mr Puzzle.' Gabriel opened the door and they all walked into the steamy, noisy kitchen.

The big chef looked up. 'Ah!' he exclaimed, and then sang out a lot of Italian. He seemed delighted to see them.

Mr Puzzle bounded over to Luigi, who bent and patted his head, saying, 'Ciao, Puzzly!'

The weasel began a long explanation in what the children presumed was Italian. They couldn't understand a word, but when Mr Puzzle waved a paw at Tom, they got the gist of it.

Luigi stared at Tom, gave an agonised moan and grabbed the boy's hand in both of his. He followed this with a stream of Italian, his voice rising and falling in a sort of wail.

'Don't!' Tom snatched his hand away. There were tears in his eyes and he began to shake his head in distress. 'What happened to my sisters?'

By now, the other kitchen staff had gathered round the children. A small dark-haired girl and two young men chattered away in Italian. Another two girls, both tall and fair, murmured and smiled, and two black men in red shirts and trousers talked excitedly in a sing-song sort of French. Mr Puzzle spoke to them in different languages and they looked at Tom, some clutching their mouths, others with wide eyes, shaking their heads in dismay.

Tom stamped his foot. 'Don't just stare at me,' he said. 'I want to see my sisters.'

'Come with me,' said Mr Puzzle.

The children followed the weasel through the kitchen, to a narrow staircase in the corner. Mr Puzzle bounded up the steps, while Tom, Gabriel, Sadie and then Lucy climbed after him in single file.

When they came to the top, Mr Puzzle told them there was yet another staircase to mount. They turned a corner and up they went. This stairwell was very dark and the steps creaked eerily beneath their feet. They tried to tiptoe, but even then the old wooden treads screeched and groaned in distress.

'We might fall right through in a minute,' Sadie whispered.

'I'll fall through first,' said Gabriel, 'I'm the biggest.'

'Sssh!' hissed Mr Puzzle. 'We're there!' And he leapt out of sight.

One by one the children stepped into the light, such as it was. They found themselves at the end of a long, shadowy corridor.

'Door on the right, halfway down,' said Mr Puzzle in a hushed, weasely voice. 'Keep to the wall – just in case.'

Staying in single file, the children began to tiptoe down the corridor.

Suddenly the weasel froze. 'Dog!' he squealed.

Everyone stopped moving. Had Dr Loth's monster dogs recovered already?

Sadie, peering round Gabriel, saw the dog at the far end of the corridor. It was standing beneath a wall-light: a medium-sized black and white dog, with tiny ears, a flat nose and small, squinty eyes.

'Oh, no!' whispered Sadie. 'It's Cecily's son, Carver.'

'It's a BOY?' cried Tom and Lucy.

'*Was*, obviously,' said Sadie. 'She did it to shut him up. He was always arguing with his brother.'

The dog curled back its lip and began to snarl.

CHAPTER NINE
The Silent Sisters

Mr Puzzle was shivering with fear. 'Dog! Dog!' he kept squeaking. 'It'll kill me.'

'No it won't,' said Gabriel. He leapt past Tom, picked up the weasel and tucked him under his arm. Running to the nearest door he opened it and beckoned the others to follow.

They all dashed into the room beyond and Gabriel slammed the door behind them – just in time, for the dog had begun to race towards them, its snarl growing meaner and louder every second.

They stood in the dark room, not daring to turn on a light.

Gabriel gently put Mr Puzzle back on his feet.

Tom asked if the dog could speak.

Sadie shrugged. 'When the sorceress lived with us –'

'She *lived* with you?' Tom's mouth dropped open.

'For a while,' said Sadie, trying to sound as though it was the most normal thing in the world. 'My dad married her, by mistake of course. She turned her son Carver into a dog to stop him bullying his brother. But then he barked and whined like any other bad-tempered dog. He's usually following his brother around.'

Tom stared at her in awe, so did Mr Puzzle.

'I was never scared of dogs before,' he said. 'It must be a weasel's instinct.'

'Anyone would be scared of *that* one,' said Tom.

Carver began to scratch the door. He barked several times and then gave a low growl.

Feeling their way in the dark, the children retreated, as far from the scratching as possible. It seemed only a matter of time before someone heard Carver's frantic barking and came to investigate. They passed the ends of six single beds and crawled under the last one.

'Year five dormitory,' Mr Puzzle squeaked, darting in beside the children.

Crouching side by side they listened to the continual barking and scratching of the angry dog.

'What do we do if someone looks in?' whispered Lucy.

'Stay where we are,' said Gabriel.

'They'll wonder why Carver wants to get in here,' said Sadie.

'Perhaps they'll think he smelled a rat,' said Gabriel.

Sadie stifled a giggle.

All at once Carver's barking stopped. There was a long, pitiful whimper, and then silence. No one said a word. Everyone had the same thought. The sorceress was in the corridor outside, frightening Carver, no doubt. Any minute now she would look into the room and turn on the light.

They waited, holding their breaths.

There was a soft creak. They expected to hear footsteps. None came. They waited and waited.

Gabriel cautiously poked his head round the bed. He could see that someone had opened the door. Light from the corridor spilled into the room.

Gabriel withdrew his head. 'Can't see anyone.' His whisper was almost inaudible. The others leaned closer, straining their ears.

'No one there,' Gabriel whispered again.

'There must be,' said Lucy.

They waited for another five minutes, but there was no sound in the room.

'I can't bear it,' Sadie said in her normal voice, and she crawled from under the bed. 'It's true,' she said. 'There's no one here. Honestly.'

'But the door opened.' Gabriel crawled out and stood beside her.

Together they walked up to the door and looked out. Carver lay before them. He was on his side, his eyes glazed, his mouth hanging open, his great tongue lolling out.

Tom and Lucy had crept up behind them. 'Is he dead?' asked Tom.

'No, I can see a heartbeat,' said Gabriel.

Sadie frowned. 'We've seen other dogs like this.'

Both at the same time, Gabriel and Sadie looked down the corridor. They saw a thin, hooded figure, a faint green glimmer, and then it was drifting down the staircase.

'He came back,' Sadie said softly. 'He hasn't deserted us.'

'No.' Gabriel never imagined he could be so happy to see a Sleeper.

Mr Puzzle's nose was twitching. 'What was *that*?' he said.

Gabriel hesitated. 'I'll explain later,' he whispered.

Before they crept back into the dormitory, Lucy suggested they bring the dog in with them. 'Someone might see it,' she said.

Gabriel tried not to show that he didn't fancy the task, but Sadie guessed. 'You keep a look out, Gabe,' she said, 'and I'll tug him in by his legs.'

Tom and Lucy screwed up their noses and backed away, but it took Sadie two seconds to pull Carver into the room. She left him, just inside the door, his tongue still lolling and his eyes holding a sort of out-of-world expression. After all the trouble Carver had caused her father, Sadie couldn't feel sorry for the insensible dog, after all he wasn't dead. She joined the others, sitting on the furthest bed.

Gabriel had decided that it was time to explain things to Mr Puzzle. 'It's like this,' he told the weasel, who had jumped up beside him. 'I had a very good reason for coming here with Tom.'

Mr Puzzle put his head on one side, eagerly awaiting the next piece of the story. And so Gabriel went back to the very beginning. He told the weasel about his unfortunate journey with the false Albert, Uncle Jack's terrible marriage, Cecily Fork's dreadful spell, the arrival of the phantom Sleepers and how his own seventh sense had brought him to Ludgarth Hall.

Mr Puzzle wore a look of rapt attention. 'You saw it all in a hat, you say? Well, well. And the precious garment that was stolen, it's obviously a great and treasured secret. I won't inquire further. But, my word, something *must* be done about it.'

'Can you help us, Mr Puzzle?' asked Sadie. 'We don't really know how to go about it.'

'Of course, I'll do everything I can,' said Mr Puzzle. 'I might be a weasel, but that gives me certain advantages.'

The door suddenly opened and the light went on.

They all dived under the bed and there was a loud scream that continued for several seconds before Mr Puzzle leapt back up.

The screaming stopped and Mr Puzzle said something in a language the children didn't understand. A woman's voice replied and then there was a dragging, scuffling sound and a giggle before the door was closed again.

'You can come out now, children,' said Mr Puzzle. 'It's quite safe.'

Gabriel was the first to crawl out. 'Who was that?' he asked.

'Yuna, one of the Mongolians kitchen helpers,' said Mr Puzzle. 'I told her the dog had fallen ill, and we didn't want it to be found up here. She's taking it outside.'

'Carver's a heavy dog,' said Sadie.

'She's a big girl, is Yuna,' said Mr Puzzle, 'very strong. She won't tell anyone where she found the dog. Those poor things in the kitchen, I think they'd all like to leave this place as soon as they get the chance.'

Tom said, plaintively, 'Are we going to find my sisters now?'

'Of course,' said Mr Puzzle. 'Follow me.'

They found a small pile of towels in the corridor. Yuna had obviously dropped them when she saw Carver.

'Clean,' Mr Puzzle observed. 'Someone had better take them to the linen room.'

'After we've found my sisters,' said Tom.

'Yes, yes.' The weasel bounded across the corridor, ran halfway down and then stopped outside another door. 'This is the room,' he whispered.

Gabriel gathered up the towels and they all crept after the weasel. Tom opened the door and switched on the light.

They looked into another empty dormitory. Six narrow beds covered in blue blankets. Six chairs and six small bedside cupboards. A bare light bulb hung in the centre of the room, giving it a cold, bleak look.

'Where *are* they?' cried Tom.

'Ssssh!' hissed the others. But Tom couldn't be silenced. He dissolved into tears, and they had to hurry into the dormitory and close the door.

Mr Puzzle scratched the fur on his chest. 'This is the room.' He scratched some more. 'I'm sure of it. I was at the far end of the corridor. I know Cecily didn't see me, because I was already in my weasel state. There were two Listeners with her. They pushed the girls in here and – ah, I remember now.'

'What? Tom begged. 'What do you remember, Mr Puzzle?'

'They locked the door,' said the weasel.

'Of course. They would have to, wouldn't they?' Gabriel remarked.

'So they've been moved,' said Lucy. 'I wish I had a phone. I could contact Mum. I know she would do something.'

Mr Puzzle gave a sudden jump. 'Phone!' he said. 'I have one, or I did have one.'

They all looked at him.

'On my desk, next floor down. In my office.'

'Can you show me, Mr Puzzle?' Gabriel was already at the door.

The weasel bounded up to him. 'Quickly, then. Take the towels. If you're seen pretend you're one of the staff, and you're taking towels to the linen room. No time to lose.'

'Yes, yes, then I can ring Mum,' Lucy said happily.

Sadie clasped her hands. 'Poor Hetty Bean. I almost forgot her. I could contact her if I knew her number.'

'Getting a phone is a good start,' said Gabriel. He stepped into the corridor.

Mr Puzzle bounded along with Gabriel running behind him. Down they went, into the dark stairwell, and then out into the brighter corridor below.

The weasel suddenly sat up, his whiskers twitching. 'Unfortunately, my office is right at the end,' he whispered.

'I'm ready,' said Gabriel.

This time the weasel moved more cautiously. They could hear footsteps and voices coming from the far end of the corridor.

'They're on the main stairs,' squeaked the weasel.

'Shall we go back?' Gabriel whispered.

'No time.' Mr Puzzle disappeared under a low table bearing a lamp.

'But . . .' Gabriel stood alone, panic-stricken. There was nowhere to hide. He couldn't possibly have squeezed under the table.

'Linen room on your left,' hissed the weasel.

Not close enough. Gabriel would have to walk another few metres before he reached another room.

And here came the Listeners – two of them, a man and a woman, both in black suits. Would they recognise him if they had been in the market? Gabriel ducked his head and moved forward.

The two strangers stopped beside Gabriel, and the man peered into his face. 'I didn't know there were any students up here. What are you doing, lurking in corridors?'

Gabriel gritted his teeth and held up the towels.

'He's working here,' said the woman. She had white hair pulled back into a ponytail, revealing her large ears.

Gabriel nodded, smiled and, remembering some

Italian he had heard, muttered, 'Si! Si!'

'Italian,' said the woman.

'So it would seem,' said the man, whose ears were even more impressive than the woman's. 'I didn't know the doctor hired them so young.'

They passed on, and Gabriel quickly ran down to what he hoped was the linen room. He opened the door and turned on the light. The room was lined with shelves of sheets, towels and blankets. An ironing board stood in the centre, and there was a rack of clothes beneath the high window. Gabriel put the towels on a shelf and was about to leave when he saw something that made him catch his breath.

Hanging at the end of the clothes rack was a grey tweed coat. Gabriel recognised it immediately. It belonged to the false Albert. It had an identical fur collar and the same large horn buttons. But this coat had been horribly damaged. The hem looked as if it had been chewed, and the cuffs hung in shreds. What terrible accident had befallen the false Albert?

Gabriel's hand was shaking when he left the room. He hadn't touched the coat and yet the terror within it had somehow leaked into him. Forgetting the weasel and his mission to find a phone, Gabriel wandered to the end of the long corridor. A wide wooden stairway led into the darkness. Holding tight to the banister, Gabriel stepped shakily down the stairs until he reached another corridor. Here the flames of a rush light in an iron bracket sent a glimmering glow across the bare stone walls.

Gabriel found himself lured, inexplicably, towards the flame. He moved slowly, reluctantly, but couldn't avoid its curious power. When he reached the light, his gaze was drawn to a door directly opposite. It was a small door with bands of iron criss-crossing the dark, pitted wood. Gabriel put his fingers on the brass handle and turned it.

He pushed the door, and its opening creak chilled his spine. There was no light in the room, nor any means of finding one, but the glow from the corridor showed him a room full of small, ancient-looking desks. Gabriel's willing feet took him to a chair before one of the desks and he sank on to its cold, hard surface.

There was a dusty cape thrown over the back and Gabriel, unable to stop himself, pulled it round his shoulders. As soon as he did this a man in a long purple robe appeared. His face was dark and lined, his straggling hair chalk white. He waved his long pale finger in the air. Were those Latin words that he was intoning?

Gabriel's seventh sense was drawing him into another boy's life, a boy who had lived at least a hundred years ago. He felt immensely tired, as though he'd been sitting here for hours, listening to the droning voice of this professor or whatever he was. Gabriel folded his arms on the desk, laid his head on them, and fell asleep.

He might have been asleep for hours or only seconds, he couldn't tell, but a light touch on his shoulder woke him. A voice, close to his ear, yet far, far away, said, 'Wake! Wake!'

Gabriel sat up. He breathed in the sweet, musky scent that he had come to know. The terrible room was bathed in a soft green light, and Etzel stood before him. 'Dear Keeper,' he said, 'thou shouldst not put thy senses in the way of beguilement, not in this place. 'Tis too strong for thee. Come!'

Gabriel got to his feet, his knees shaking, and followed Etzel out of the dreadful room. The phantom led him to the staircase and pointed to the top. 'Thy friend awaits,' he said.

Gabriel wanted to know more. 'The cloak,' he said. 'Do you know if it's here? Am I in the right place?'

Etzel looked bewildered. 'It is not for me to know this. I must accompany thee, help thee wheresoever thou goest.' He scratched his head. 'Thou hath the seventh sense. Thou hast employed it?'

'It led me here,' said Gabriel.

'Then here it must be.' Etzel smiled. 'Unless thy

sense hath failed thee?'

Had it failed him? For the second time Gabriel began to doubt his seventh sense. 'But Erebus drove me here,' he insisted. 'So he must know.'

Etzel stroked his narrow chin. 'Not so,' he said. 'Erebus drives thee to search for the cloak, but there are times when he hath no knowledge of its hiding place.'

'I see.' Gabriel was puzzled. He began to mount the stairs, and when he looked back the phantom was beginning to fade.

'Etzel,' Gabriel called. 'Where do you go, when you . . .?'

The phantom spread his hands. 'I sleep,' came the weary voice, and he vanished.

Mr Puzzle was waiting for Gabriel at the top of the stairs. 'Where've you been?' he said crossly. 'Who were you talking to?'

'I got lost,' said Gabriel. 'The phantom helped me.'

'Huh!' said Mr Puzzle. 'People are stirring. We can't hang about. My office is right here.' He leapt away.

Gabriel followed, his heart thumping in his chest. Voices could be heard, but they managed to reach the door to Mr Puzzle's office before anyone else appeared.

'Look on the desk,' said the weasel. 'I'm sure I

left it there.'

Once inside Gabriel switched on the light and closed the door. He found himself in a very untidy room. It was cluttered with musical instruments, piles of manuscripts and four music stands. The huge desk was littered with paper and jars of pens and pencils.

'Nice, isn't it?' said Mr Puzzle.

Gabriel thought the weasel was being sarcastic, but he clearly wasn't, as he added, 'I love it in here. At least I used to, when I could get in and out.'

'It can't be easy, being so changed,' said Gabriel as he rummaged around on the desk. Sheaves of paper, loose pens and books slipped to the floor as Gabriel delved deeper into the mess on Mr Puzzle's desk.

'No, it's impossible, said Mr Puzzle. 'I was happy here, you know. I have this nice office, and the pupils love singing.' He sighed. 'Of course I'll have to leave now that she's come here, whether I'm a weasel or not.' He began to scrabble about on the floor. 'Can you see the phone on the desk?'

'I don't think it's here,' said Gabriel.

'It is. It must be.' The weasel leapt on to the chair which revolved twice very fast, before coming to rest, facing the desk again. 'Drat it, I forgot that,' said the weasel. He jumped from the chair to the desk and began to scratch about with his claws. 'Here it is,' he squeaked, his nose in a pile of papers.

Gabriel pulled the mobile out of the muddle. 'It doesn't have much battery left,' he remarked.

'Never mind. One call is all you need.' Mr Puzzle leapt off the desk. 'Let's go.'

When they left the office, the voices from below seemed closer, but luckily no one appeared as Gabriel and the weasel made a dash for the stairs.

Back in the dormitory they found the girls looking very glum. Tom had a tear-stained face.

'We thought you'd been caught,' said Sadie.

'And then what would we do?' said Lucy.

Gabriel handed her the phone. 'It hasn't got much battery left,' he told her. 'Just tell your mum not to worry and . . . and that you'll be back tomorrow. Oh, and if she happens to see a large woman in a red coat, who looks a bit desperate, and might even be at the police station by now . . .'

'Her name's Hetty Bean,' Sadie said quickly.

'Why can't I get Mum to come up right now?' said Lucy.

'She'd never get in,' Mr Puzzle told her. 'It's too dangerous. We'll find a way to get you out in the morning. I'll have a word with your mum, Lucy, put her mind at rest. After all, she can't see what happened to me.'

When Lucy got through to her mother, she told her everything that the others had suggested, and then she held the phone in front of Mr Puzzle's face. He reassured Mrs Bright, saying that Lucy and her new friends, Sadie and Gabriel, were staying the night at the hall, and would return in the morning.

'Mr Puzzle,' Mrs Bright raised her voice and they all heard her say, 'Hetty Bean is here, with me. I met her in the police station. What a coincidence, she'll be so relieved to know where the children are. But are you sure it's safe?'

'I'll take good care of them,' said Mr Puzzle. 'They've got nice, comfy beds, and you shouldn't come up here in the dark, what with those big dogs about.'

'Well, if you're sure –' The voice was cut off as the phone died.

'What luck that Hetty met Lucy's mum,' cried Sadie. 'She can let Dad know, and no one will worry about us.'

'But we're NOT safe,' Tom moaned. 'And where are my sisters? I want to see them.'

Mr Puzzle tried to persuade Tom to wait for the morning, but Tom just hunched his shoulders and cupped his face in his hands.

'Nothing more can be done now,' said the weasel. People are coming to bed. You'll have to sleep in here for the night.'

'I want to go to the bathroom,' said Tom.

As soon as the words were spoken, everyone had the same idea.

Mr Puzzle sighed. 'Too risky! Too risky!' he muttered. And then he remembered a derelict apartment at the top of the house. Dr Loth's sister, a strange recluse, had lived there until she died. 'It's a creepy place,' said the weasel. 'Dark, damp and dusty. But there's bathroom.'

Once again the children found themselves creeping after Mr Puzzle. Along endless corridors they went, stumbling on the threadbare carpeting, and squinting in the dim light. Gabriel hoped that no one was made to sleep behind some of the cobweb-covered doors they passed.

Toadstools grew on both sides of the staircase up to the empty apartment. The treads were slippery with mould, and if it hadn't been for Lucy's torch, one of them would surely have fallen.

The door at the top was grey with cobwebs, but the brass handle had been polished. They crowded on to the narrow landing while Gabriel turned the handle and pushed. The door wouldn't move.

'Must be locked,' he said, putting his shoulder to it and shoving in vain. The lock was shiny and had recently been used, he noticed.

There was a sudden patter of feet. Someone on the other side of the door tapped, again and again.

Now there were several pairs of hands, all tapping and knocking.

Mr Puzzle put a paw to his mouth. 'I wonder if the girls are *here*?' he exclaimed.

'My sisters!' cried Tom, putting his ear to the door. 'Dinah, Poppy, Leonora!' he called. 'It's Tom.'

He was answered by more frantic tapping.

'Is it you?' cried Tom. 'Why won't you answer?'

'They can't,' said Mr Puzzle.

'Why?' asked everyone at once.

The weasel sighed. 'They were struck dumb – all three. Oh, I'm sorry, so very sorry, my dears. Another of Cecily's terrible spells.'

'I must see them,' Tom demanded. 'I must.'

'Then we'll find a way,' said Sadie.

Everyone agreed. But how? The door looked so solid, so impregnable. How could they possibly open a locked door without a key? A key that was most probably in the possession of a sorceress.

'At this rate we'll never get to a bathroom,' Lucy muttered.

The others ignored her. They couldn't bring themselves to retreat from the sisters' desperate tapping. They crouched on the floor beside the heavy door, while Tom pressed his hands against the wood, telling his sisters they would soon be free, soon talking again. How Dinah would be telling him stories, how Poppy would be singing and Leonora dancing, and how they would all go home and eat the turkey he had cooked completely by himself on Christmas Day.

Gabriel thought, sooner or later, someone is going to hear Tom's chatter, and we'll pay for it. He clasped his arms across his chest and waited.

A familiar, spicy scent drifted about him in the damp, gloomy air. A green light glimmered on the staircase and came closer.

CHAPTER TEN
False Albert's Coat

Gabriel stood up. 'Etzel?' he whispered.

The others turned and watched the light grow stronger. Lifeless insects floated in the rising glimmer, and then the phantom appeared.

The girls slowly got to their feet and Sadie asked, 'Have you come to help us, Etzel?'

The phantom gazed steadily at Gabriel. 'Keeper,' he said, 'thou dost tarry here.'

'Tarry?' Gabriel repeated.

'He means you're delaying,' Sadie informed him.

'Of course,' Gabriel mumbled. 'Forgive me, Etzel, but my friend here seeks his lost sisters.'

'Sisters? Lost?' Etzel regarded Tom with a look of compassion.

'I think I have found them,' said Tom, keeping his hand pressed against the door. 'But they're locked in here, and we can't get the key.'

'Key?' The phantom stepped up to the door and

the children were enclosed in his soft green mist.

At that moment the knocking from the other side of the door began again, and Tom, who hadn't left his post, tapped back.

'Dinah, Poppy, Leonora, we're still here.' His voice had softened in the phantom's presence but it was loud enough, for the knocking became stronger and faster.

'They do not speak,' Etzel remarked.

'A spell,' said a voice at the phantom's foot. Etzel frowned and looked down at the weasel. Mr Puzzle returned the phantom's stare. 'Tom's poor sisters were struck dumb by a sorceress,' he said.

'And yet a weasel speaketh?' said Etzel.

'Another spell,' Mr Puzzle muttered.

'Spells must be undone!' Etzel declared and his pale hand passed so swiftly over the lock, it appeared to be nothing more than a fleeting moonbeam.

The door swung open and the three girls behind it backed away, their hands pressed to their mouths.

Etzel made a low bow and stood aside as Tom ran into the room, crying, 'He's just a phantom, he won't hurt you.'

The three sisters hugged and stroked their little brother, but not a sound passed their lips, and they still glanced anxiously at Etzel in the doorway. One of the girls was tall and dark – Tom addressed her as Dinah. Poppy had red hair like Tom's and the smallest girl, who had long tangles of chestnut hair, was Leonora.

'Come and meet my sisters.' Tom beckoned the others.

While they stepped cautiously into the room, Etzel slowly began to disappear, but not before Sadie became aware that he was staring at her. It was almost as if he knew her.

Perhaps I remind him of his sister, Sadie thought. She would have asked Etzel but by then he had completely vanished. She wished he had stayed a little longer with them.

Tom made all the introductions and his sisters smiled and nodded, but they still looked anxious and uncertain. It didn't help that Tom kept asking why they had been struck dumb, because it was quite clear they couldn't tell him.

'You saw something, didn't you?' said Gabriel. 'Something you weren't supposed to see.'

All three sisters nodded, vehemently.

'What did you see?' begged Tom. 'What? What?'

The girls looked at him sadly.

Lucy felt in her pocket and withdrew a crumpled piece of paper and a pencil. She held them out to Dinah, who grimaced and shook her head. Poppy did the same.

'Why won't you write it?' Tom pleaded. 'What's wrong?'

'Perhaps they *can't* write it,' Sadie suggested.

'Can't you? Can't you?'

Suddenly, Leonora snatched the pencil and paper and ran to a small table. She smoothed the paper and began to write. But before she had finished even one letter, the pencil flew out of her hand.

Tom picked it up and handed it back to her. This time, as soon as Leonora touched the pencil it broke in two, and her hand began to shake so much she couldn't even touch it.

'This is a wicked spell indeed,' said Mr Puzzle.

The sisters hadn't noticed the little weasel until that moment, and they stared at him in amazement.

'You know the voice, my dears,' said Mr Puzzle. 'It's me, the choirmaster. I was helping with the carol singing. This was done to me because I said what I shouldn't have, and I believe that you saw or heard what you shouldn't have.'

The girls grimaced. Dinah lifted her shoulders in a huge sigh, but not a sound escaped her. Poppy looked hopelessly at the floor, and tears trickled down Leonora's freckled cheeks.

'We'll make you better,' Tom declared. 'Won't we, Gabriel?'

'Mmm,' mumbled Gabriel, trying to give the girls

an assured smile, but not having a clue how he could undo such malicious work.

None of them heard the soft footfalls on the steps, and the sudden appearance of a very large stranger took them all by surprise. It was one of the African men they had first seen in the kitchen. He carried a tray of food and wore a long blue apron over his red shirt and trousers. His red velvet slippers were patterned with golden stars, and round his neck hung a brass key on a silver chain.

When he saw the open door and the children gathered inside, he uttered several loud, unintelligible words. His voice was becoming quite thunderous when the weasel leapt forward and pacified him.

The weasel's words brought a big smile to the stranger's face. He laid the tray on the floor, gave a conspiratorial shrug and crept away on his wonderfully soft slippers.

'I like those slippers,' Lucy murmured. 'And he didn't even slip on those steps.'

The weasel frowned at her, as if this was no time to be admiring slippers. 'Mutara won't breathe a word,' he said. 'He's a great friend of mine.'

They all found themselves staring at the contents of the tray: three plates of sliced salami, hunks of cheese and slices of bread and butter – a feast for hungry children.

Tom seized a piece of salami, but before he could take another Sadie warned him that the food belonged to his sisters, who were probably even hungrier than he was.

'For a whole day I've only had a piece of turkey that I cooked all by myself,' said Tom, but he picked up the tray and carried it over to the table. 'When you've had your supper, we can all go home,' he told his sisters. 'There's lots of food there, and the turkey that I cooked.'

Dinah smiled at Tom and sadly shook her head.

'Don't do that,' said Tom. 'The door's not locked; we can leave this place right now.'

'Tom, you can't,' said Gabriel. 'It's pitch dark for one thing, and the sorceress might catch you.'

'I want to go home as much as you do,' said Lucy, 'but now I'm scared of being turned into something else.'

Tom stamped his foot. 'The sorceress won't see us if it's dark.'

'Ssssh!' hissed the others.

Sadie reminded Tom that only the sorceress could undo her terrible spell.

'I'll help them,' said Tom, beginning to sob again.

Dinah came and hugged him until he stopped. Then she took him to the table where she carefully divided the food into seven portions and held it out to the others. Leonora pointed at the weasel, but Mr Puzzle assured her that he could find food very easily. He had good connections in the kitchen.

Tom took some food and began to eat it immediately. The other three hung back, not wanting to deprive the silent sisters of their meal. Dinah, now smiling, kept pushing the plates towards them. It was difficult to resist. Impossible, in fact.

When they had all eaten and visited what Lucy described as a medieval bathroom, Tom refused to leave his sisters. He would hide under one of the beds, so no prying eyes would see him. The others decided to return to one of the dormitories. Hopefully, the sorceress wouldn't look in on the sisters during the night, and discover the unlocked door.

'We'll decide what to do next in the morning,' said Mr Puzzle. 'The king's cloak must be found, that is crucial, but how this wretched spell can be undone my dears –' he turned to the three sisters – 'I cannot imagine. It's all given me quite a headache.'

'So weasels can get headaches,' said Lucy, thoughtfully.

The weasel's head swivelled in her direction, but he didn't reply. Instead he bounded to the door and, after bidding Tom and his sisters goodnight, the others followed him.

They were halfway down the dangerous staircase

when a spine-chilling shriek stopped them in their tracks. Doors opened and slammed. Voices called up the stairs, and heavy feet pounded the corridor below.

'What's going on?' shouted a woman very close to the motionless children.

Another voice gave a long rambling answer but they couldn't make out the words.

'The dog?' said the woman. 'Eben, we'd better go down, Cecily's in a state. Her dog has been attacked.'

'Like the other two?' asked the man.

'Probably. Come on. There's a canine assassin about.'

The children searched each others' faces in the gloom. Sadie grimaced, Lucy's mouth dropped open and Gabriel whispered, 'Those dogs weren't dead. They were just . . . sort of . . . frozen, temporarily, Etzel said.'

All at once, Mr Puzzle leapt down into the corridor, bounded across to the back stairs and disappeared.

'He's deserted us,' mouthed Lucy.

Gabriel shook his head. He couldn't believe that Mr Puzzle was showing signs of real weaseliness.

They didn't dare to move. The noise below was getting louder. Were Cecily and her Listeners searching for the perpetrator, the slayer of her least favourite son?

Tom poked his head round the door and whispered, 'What's happening?'

Gabriel shooed him back, murmuring, 'Not safe,' under his breath.

Tom retreated, looking scared, and closed the door.

The hullabaloo continued for at least an hour, by which time Lucy had fallen asleep on Sadie's shoulder, Sadie was nodding off and Gabriel had to keep telling himself to stay awake, or they would all tumble into the corridor.

When every sound had died away, he judged that it was safe for them to nip along to the nearest dormitory. He tapped Sadie's knee, and she gave Lucy a little shake. Lucy squeaked. She had forgotten where she was and, in a frightened voice, began to ask what was happening.

Sadie put her fingers over Lucy's mouth and gave her a whispered explanation.

'I remember,' muttered Lucy. 'I'd love to sleep in a real bed.'

The three children tottered shakily down to the bottom of the stairs, crept along to the next staircase and eventually to the dormitory they had found before. They each chose a bed, pulled the blankets over their heads and fell asleep, almost immediately.

Gabriel wasn't sure how long he had slept, but he woke up well before dawn. Something tugged at his mind. He kept seeing the false Albert's torn coat. What had happened to him? Gabriel had to find out, and there was only one way to do that. He must put on the coat.

The idea appalled him. He tried to resist it, terrified of what might have happened to Albert, and what would happen to *him* if he put on the coat. But if it brought him closer to the king's cloak, then it had to be done.

Gabriel slipped out of bed and felt his way to the door. The girls slept on, Lucy moaning a little, Sadie muttering in her dreams. Gabriel let himself into the corridor and closed the door. He remembered that the linen room was on the next floor down, close to Mr Puzzle's office.

Tiptoeing to the back stairs, Gabriel crept down to the next floor. Small wall lights illumined the corridor and he soon found the room he wanted. Taking a deep breath, Gabriel opened the door, slid inside and put on the light. There was the coat, hanging at the end of the rack. Gabriel nervously approached it. He touched the fur collar, the torn sleeves, and his whole body recoiled from the contact. To wear that coat was the last thing in the world that Gabriel wanted to do. And yet he must.

When he took the coat from its hanger, he found that it was heavy and damp. It dragged at his hands and he let it drop to the floor. Slowly Gabriel hauled the coat up and drew it round his shoulders. After a moment's hesitation he pushed his arms into the sleeves. The torn hem touched the floor and chilled his bare feet. The moist weight of it pulled at his shoulders. But then an unfamiliar strength seeped into his bones. He began to feel taller and wider, just as he had when he had worn the black hat. Gabriel closed his eyes.

If he had been cold before, now he was freezing. He was making his way along a snowy lane. Icy flakes flew in his face, almost blinding him. His head was bare and the arctic temperature numbed his nose and his ears. The wind was tugging at a small leather bag that he carried. He tucked it under his arm to keep it safe.

All at once a cloud of snow swept towards him. It battered his head and his body, it tore at his hands and whipped his legs. He clutched the bag closer, but the snowstorm pulled and pushed, it froze his fingers and tore the bag from his grasp.

'No,' he moaned. 'Not the cloak!' The voice belonged to the false Albert.

There came an answer in the wind, a high, wintry wail, 'Not thine, thief!'

The man Gabriel had become fell to his knees in the snow. His bag was gone. Cradled in the arms of the snow it was travelling over white fields and hedges, far from thieves and Fork sorcery.

Gabriel's body ached from its icy battering. As he staggered to his feet, he was caught in the headlights of a large vehicle: a jeep, its wheels encased in chains, crunching against the snow. It stopped and a man in a duffel coat jumped out.

'Is that you, Amos?' called the man.

Gabriel found himself groaning, 'Mmm.'

'We got your call. Where's the bag?'

'I don't know, Cutter,' Gabriel replied. 'It's here, somewhere. The wind tore it out of my arms.'

Cutter swore. He produced a torch. 'It can't have gone far. We'll have to look for it.' He called to someone in the jeep. 'Jake, we've got work to do.'

The passenger door opened and another man jumped out. He wore a yellow mac and a waterproof cowboy hat.

'Amos lost the bag,' said Cutter. 'We'll have to find it before it's covered in snow.'

'Idiot!' grumbled Jake. He opened the back door of the jeep and pulled out several spades. One landed at Gabriel's feet.

He was not sure what happened next because the false Albert passed out, but the next thing he knew, he was being dragged into the great hall that he had visited when wearing the black fur hat.

Cecily Fork was standing beneath the hanging spears of the chandelier. When she turned her head, her shining, steel-grey hair was almost blinding. This time there was a man beside her – Dr Loth, thought Gabriel. A black, velvet cape hung from the man's sloping shoulders, above it his face was lined and gaunt. His thin black hair hung over his ears like a wet rag, his moustache was long and narrow, his beard a small pointed tuft. Perched on his sharp, beetroot-coloured nose was a pair of tiny round-framed spectacles, the lenses – as thick as magnifying glasses – enlarged his pine-green eyes to such an alarming extent, he looked more like a fish than a human being.

'Where is it?' the sorceress demanded, staring at Gabriel.

The false Albert was silent.

'You've hidden it, stolen it. Did you really think you could get away with it? Where were you off to when Cutter found you? Where did you HIDE it?' Cecily stamped a steel-toed boot, her voice was a grating shriek.

'It was taken,' the false Albert whined. 'The wind tore the bag out of my arms. I did everything you asked, made sure Alan Silk got the invitation to the Alchemists' Convention – I'd like to have used the invitation myself, actually.' He coughed. 'I watched, waited. I switched the cloaks, left the train, made sure the . . . thing the boy mentioned wasn't following.'

'What thing?' Cecily demanded.

'I never saw it, but the boy described it: an ancient, skeletal being, hooded, smelling of decay . . .'

Cecily's head came forward on its long white neck, her narrow eyes widening, 'WHAT? Ichabod, did you hear that? What d'you make of it?'

'Lies,' replied the doctor in an oily voice. 'The dogs will get the truth from him.' He gave a shrill whistle, and the three monstrous white dogs appeared at the back of the hall. They padded up to the man and sat, one each side of him and one at his feet.

Little do they know what's coming to them, thought Gabriel, but right now he was in the past, in the false Albert's coat, before it was chewed to bits.

'TAKE!' Dr Loth commanded, pointing at Gabriel. The dogs sprang.

Heavy jaws closed around the false Albert's wrists, sharp teeth bit into his flesh. His coat was tugged and he fell back, hitting his head on the stone floor.

'The truth, Amos! THE TRUTH!' yelled Cecily.

A few indistinct words came from Ichabod Loth. 'Take him to the laba . . .' Gabriel couldn't hear the rest. Then the doctor growled. 'You'll stay there, Amos, and do your work until we get the cloak. The dogs will find it, won't you, my beauties?'

Cecily screamed something in her bitter, acid

voice, and then the pain in Gabriel's head and the agony of his chewed hands were too much to bear, and he cried out.

CHAPTER ELEVEN
A Visit from the Weasel

'Gabe, wake up!'

Gabriel felt himself slipping out of the false Albert's life. The pain eased from the back of his head; he flexed his fingers and knew they were his own. Opening his eyes he saw that shelves of linen had replaced the dazzle of the chandelier and the steely shine of the sorceress's hair.

Gabriel breathed a long sigh of relief.

'I thought you were a goner,' said a familiar voice.

Gabriel turned his head and there was Sadie's anxious face, peering down at him. She was holding the grey coat.

'Well, congratulations,' said Sadie, dropping the coat. 'That was the scariest "other life" I've ever seen you in. Why on earth didn't you tell me what you were going to do?'

'You were asleep,' Gabriel mumbled.

'I woke up when you left the room,' said Sadie.

'I waited a bit, then I tiptoed along the corridor. I didn't dare to open any of the doors, but I remembered Mr Puzzle's office, and I thought you might have come down here. I was just passing this store room when I heard you groaning.'

Gabriel sat up. 'I saw his coat, Sadie. I had to put it on.'

'Whose coat?'

'The false Albert's, the man who stole the cloak. His real name is Amos.'

'Oh, I see.' Sadie crouched beside Gabriel. 'Did the coat tell you anything?'

'Yes . . . and no.' In a hushed voice Gabriel told Sadie everything he had experienced of false Albert's journey through the snow, and later in the great hall.

'*Snow* took the cloak?' Sadie's whisper was full of questions. 'But how?'

Gabriel shrugged. 'The bag was snatched away, the snow and the wind carried it off.'

For several seconds, Sadie was silent, and then she said again, 'The snow?'

Gabriel leaned closer to her, frowning. 'What are you thinking, Sadie?'

Sadie gave him a mysterious smile. 'I don't really know. It's just – I have a strange feeling about the snow.'

Gabriel stared at her. 'The cloak's not here. I know

that now. But where did the snow take it, Sadie?'

'Who knows? But if the cloak's not here, we'd better get out as soon as we can. You've only got three days left to find it, Gabe.'

'*Three days*,' Gabriel shuddered. 'And then what?' he murmured.

They got to their feet and Gabriel hung the coat back on the rack. The touch of the damp wool made him shiver.

Sadie was about to open the door when they heard voices.

'It came from somewhere along here,' said a voice thick with phlegm.

'Under the shelves, Sadie.' Gabriel quickly switched off the light and they squeezed themselves under the shelves of linen.

They were only just in time. A second later the door opened.

'I thought it came from here,' snuffled a voice that Gabriel recognised. 'It was a horrible groaning noise.'

'It could be in Puzzle's room.' This sounded like the man who had driven the jeep when Gabriel was Amos.

'Who's Puzzle?' asked the other man.

'A weasel,' said Cutter.

'A weasel?'

Cutter gave a spiteful laugh. 'He was the choirmaster. Silly man, always putting his foot in it.'

The other man chuckled. 'One of Cecily's victims? He's hardly likely to come back to his room then, is he?'

'You never know.'

The light went out and the door was closed. Heavy footsteps faded down the corridor.

Sadie and Gabriel waited until they could hear only the thump of their own hearts, then they crept back to the dormitory. Lucy was still fast asleep.

Gabriel woke again to the sound of scratching. Outside the uncurtained windows, the dark sky showed streaks of yellowy-grey. Gabriel tiptoed to the door and put his ear against it.

'It's me,' Mr Puzzle whispered.

Gabriel flung open the door and Mr Puzzle somersaulted into the room. 'Not so fast, young man,' he panted.

'Sorry, I thought you were in a hurry,' said Gabriel.

'Well, I don't want to be seen, do I? You just took me by surprise. I thought you were all asleep.'

'Some of us are,' said Gabriel, looking at the beds occupied by Sadie and Lucy.

'My claws are getting quite worn down,' complained Mr Puzzle. 'Wherever I go, I have to keep scratching at doors.'

'That must be very annoying,' Gabriel

commiserated, 'but perhaps you won't always have claws.'

Mr Puzzle gave him a hopeful look and asked if they'd all slept well. By now the girls were waking up. While Gabriel told the weasel about his journey in the black coat, Sadie kept yawning and Lucy never stopped gasping.

'So where d'you think they took him?' asked Lucy. 'The man in the damp coat?'

Gabriel rubbed his head. 'I'm not sure. It sounded like *laba*, or *labor*. Something like that. I couldn't hear it all.'

'Lab!' Mr Puzzle exclaimed. 'If it's Amos Arkwright he'll be back in his laboratory. He's something of an alchemist. I'm told he's trying to turn wood-pulp into steel for the doctor. But who knows? I'm forgetting,' he went on. 'Something unfortunate has occurred.'

The children waited for the bad news, Sadie demanding, 'Tell us, then. Tell us!'

The weasel looked regretfully at the children. 'My friend, Luigi, tells me that a guard has been posted at every exit. So, for now, it will be impossible for any of you to get out of this place.'

'But Mum's expecting me!' cried Lucy. 'Why are there guards all round the hall?'

Mr Puzzle spread his paws. 'Dogs have been

robbed of their strength, there were groans in the night. Dr Loth suspects intruders. Cecily thinks it's something supernatural.'

'We'd better keep well hidden,' said Gabriel.

Lucy spluttered, 'But . . . but . . . but . . .'

'We'll find a way –' the weasel looked at Gabriel – 'won't we, Gabriel?'

'I suppose so,' Gabriel said lamely.

Mr Puzzle looked a little disappointed, but he said, 'I have a plan. Since you are all prisoners, I shall go and see Lucy's mum myself, and put her mind at rest.'

'It won't make Mum happy to know I'm a prisoner,' Lucy pointed out, rather ungratefully.

'Or to meet a talking weasel,' Sadie added before she could stop herself. 'And anyway, how will you get out, Mr Puzzle?'

'Easy,' said the weasel, ignoring Sadie's first remark. 'After breakfast I'll get into the big pocket in Luigi's apron, and when he goes outside to the bins, I'll jump down and crawl through the long grass. Luigi will keep the guard talking, and I'll never be seen.'

'But if someone in the town sees you, they might hurt you,' said Lucy.

This seemed to irritate Mr Puzzle who said impatiently, 'This is the very reason that I haven't been successful before. D'you think I haven't tried to warn people, to make contact? Someone actually kicked me! But children are different, they pay more attention to small animals, and you have a brother and sister, Lucy.'

'I wouldn't rely on them.' Lucy said this quite innocently, but Mr Puzzle seemed to take offence on Lucy's siblings' behalf. 'You should give them more credit,' he said severely.

Lucy flushed and Sadie said quickly, 'I think it's an excellent idea, Mr Puzzle, and if you see Hetty, can you make sure she rings my dad?'

'Naturally,' the weasel replied, 'but no doubt she already has.'

Before Mr Puzzle left them, Gabriel asked if Mutara could possibly bring them a tiny bit of breakfast. 'Perhaps,' Gabriel suggested, 'on his way up to the silent sisters he could bring us some toast, and maybe an egg?'

'Porridge for me,' said Sadie, and Lucy added, 'A spot of bacon?'

'You don't want much, do you?' said the weasel. 'You're supposed to keep hidden, but I'll see what I can do.'

When Mr Puzzle had gone, three glum children contemplated a long, dreary day ahead. The only high point would be a hot breakfast, and even that was just a possibility.

'Nothing in this world is certain,' said Sadie with a sigh.

Lucy's brother, Johnny, was leaning on his front gate. It was still very cold; almost too cold for snow, someone had said, and indeed the snow had eased off in the night. Now a fresh wind blew across the banks of snow, sending little flurries of ice into Johnny's face. It was still better than being inside, though. His mother and Hetty Bean hadn't stopped talking about the missing children all morning.

What had happened to them? Why hadn't they come back? What was going on up at the hall? Hetty Bean was all for going up there to sort things out, but Johnny's mum knew better. If three sisters had disappeared and the police wouldn't do a thing about it, something was seriously wrong.

'We'd be no use to anyone if we disappeared too, would we?' said Mrs Bright. 'I spoke to the choirmaster and Lucy, and they seem to be quite safe, for now.'

All his life, ever since his father had run off, Johnny had tried to do the right thing. He had kept an eye on Florence, carried the shopping for his mum, tidied Lucy's messes and attempted to stop her doing risky things. But his older sister had a mind of her own.

She never paid him any attention. Johnny was fed up with it. 'She's got what was coming to her,' he muttered into the wind.

'Hello, Johnny,' said a voice.

Johnny leaned over the gate and looked up and down the road. There was no one in sight.

'And now I'm hearing things,' he said.

'No, no,' came the voice. 'It's me. I'm here, right beside you.'

'Arrrgh!' growled Johnny. 'There's no one beside the gate. Go away, ghost, or whatever you are. I don't believe in you.'

'Look down,' the voice ordered, 'under the latch. I'm not *that* small, am I?'

Johnny wiped the melting snow away from his eyes, blinked and looked down. 'I can see a . . . a stoat?' he said cautiously.

'A weasel,' Mr Puzzle corrected.

'Am I dreaming, Mr Weasel? I am, aren't I?'

'No, Johnny. Unfortunately I am a weasel, for now,' said Mr Puzzle. 'I was formerly Mr Puzzle, the choirmaster up at Ludgarth Hall.'

Johnny decided he'd better believe what he was seeing. 'You gave concerts and stuff up there.'

'Indeed,' said Mr Puzzle. 'Look, Johnny, can I have a word with your mother?'

'Is it about Lucy?'

176

'Lucy amongst other things,' said the weasel.

'OK.' Johnny opened the gate and the weasel leapt into the garden. 'I'm not quite sure how I'm going to explain this,' said Johnny. 'You'd better stay in the hallway while I go and warn her.'

'I quite understand.'

Mr Puzzle followed Johnny up the path and remained outside the kitchen while Johnny went to alert his mother.

When he entered the kitchen his mother and Hetty Bean were standing by the stove, still talking at the tops of their voices. Poor Florence was trying to do some drawing at the table and blocking her ears with one hand at the same time.

'Mum, I've got something to tell you,' Johnny said in a loud voice.

Mrs Bright took no notice, so the next time he shouted, 'MUM, it's urgent!'

At last he had her attention. 'What is it, Johnny?' asked his mother, looking alarmed.

'Someone, er, something wants to talk to you.'

'Who? What?' said Mary Bright, frowning.

Johnny tried to choose his words carefully. 'It's . . . um . . . a weasel, but . . .'

'Oh, really, Johnny!' Mrs Bright gave a sigh of exasperation. 'Close the front door, the draught is freezing our ankles.'

Florence asked, 'Do weasels talk?'

'Of course not, love,' said Hetty Bean, patting her head.

'Well, this one DOES!' Johnny shouted. 'And he's got news of Lucy, and he's really Mr Puzzle, the choirmaster.'

Mary Bright began to look concerned. 'Johnny, you're not making sense, come and –'

At that moment Mr Puzzle leapt into the kitchen. He'd been listening to the conversation through the half-open front door and had decided it was time to make an entrance.

'Good morning!' he said.

The two women stared at him. Hetty Bean dropped a dishcloth and Florence beamed with delight. Clearing her throat, Mary Bright said huskily, 'I spoke to you last night, on the phone. Were you a weasel then?'

'Indeed.' Mr Puzzle bounded round the table and held his paws up to the glowing logs in the stove window. 'Do forgive me, but it's so chilly outside,' he said, 'and my fur is very damp.'

'I . . . I'm sure,' said Mary Bright, with a half-smile.

Hetty Bean bent closer to the weasel and asked, 'Do you have something to tell us?'

Florence piped up, 'Is it about Lucy? And did the sorceress turn you into a weasel?'

Mr Puzzle looked up at Florence with the nearest he could get to a smile on his weasel face. 'Indeed! Indeed! Right on both counts, young lady.'

Now that the situation was becoming clearer, Johnny ran to close the front door, and then everyone took a seat at the table. Mr Puzzle was invited on to it. After a few introductions, a good rubdown with a towel, and a slice of fruit cake, the weasel told them all that had befallen Tom's three sisters, and how Gabriel, Sadie and Lucy were now hiding in a dormitory, and would be quite safe – unless they were discovered.

Mr Puzzle was about to advise them on their next course of action, when Hetty Bean jumped to her feet, crying, 'We must go up to the hall. Gabriel and Sadie were in my care – I'm totally responsible!'

The weasel shook his head. 'Not a good idea, Miss Bean,' he said. 'There are guards at every entrance, and the sorceress is not above turning you all into tiny creatures – insects, even. And there you would be, lost in the woods, too small to be heard and at the mercy of much bigger creatures.'

'Such as yourself,' said Johnny.

'As if I would,' Mr Puzzle protested. 'But other weasels, naturally.'

A worried silence descended. Even Florence could find nothing to say. The weasel helped himself to another slice of cake, and then curled up on the table. He closed his eyes and before anyone could say a word, he had fallen asleep.

'Poor little thing,' said Hetty. 'He's come a long way, and he didn't have to.'

Mary Bright agreed. 'At least we know where things stand,' she said. 'But the power of that woman – I had no idea. I knew that the town councillors and even the police were not doing their duty. You could tell that they were under some sort of malign influence, and some of us did wonder if it was Cecily Fork and her "people". Listeners or whatever they are.'

'The sorceress and her apprentices,' Johnny said grimly.

Hetty asked if she could cook the lunch, to take her mind off things. 'Cooking always helps,' she said.

Mary Bright was only too happy to let someone else cook. They all set about clearing the table, and laying it for lunch, while Mr Puzzle went on dreaming, right in the centre. He didn't wake up until he smelled Hetty's delicious parsnip soup.

Hetty cooled the soup before ladling it into a large saucer, and Mr Puzzle gratefully drank it all down with a piece of toast.

'I'd better be off now,' he said, licking his lips. 'Those poor children will be worried. At the moment

I just can't think of a way to get them out, without putting them in danger.'

'Without being spellbound,' said Florence, her eyes very wide.

'Exactly.' Mr Puzzle gave her a nod and jumped off the table.

'Wait!' cried Mary Bright, as the weasel ran for the door. 'Take my mobile phone, and then Lucy can ring our home phone, whenever she gets a chance.'

Mr Puzzle looked up at her, rather sadly. He patted his body, all over, and said, 'Where would I put it?'

'Ah, yes. I see the problem.' Mary scratched her head.

'You could carry it in a bag round your neck,' Johnny suggested.

'He might strangle himself,' said Florence, 'or get caught on a bramble.'

'Risky,' Mr Puzzle agreed.

'I know!' Florence declared. 'You could wear my teddy's coat. It's just your size, and it's got pockets.' She immediately ran to fetch it, and returned with a smart, teddy-sized jacket. It had four brass buttons down the front, and two deep pockets.

Mr Puzzle regarded it doubtfully. 'It's very eye-catching,' he remarked. 'I'd rather not be seen quite so easily.'

Florence looked disappointed. 'Oh, please, just try it on.'

To please her, Mr Puzzle allowed Florence to drape the coat round his shoulders and squeeze his arms into the sleeves. They were far too long, and Florence had to roll them up before the weasel could free his paws. Then she buttoned up the coat and Johnny slipped the mobile into one of the pockets.

'Perfect,' said brother and sister.

'It looks rather fetching,' Hetty agreed.

'Good luck, Mr Puzzle,' said Mary Bright, leading him outside and opening the gate.

They all crowded behind her and waved Mr Puzzle goodbye, as he bounded away beside the hedgerows.

'So far so good,' panted the weasel, having safely reached the wood. 'Next bit might be risky.'

He was halfway up the hill when he heard voices coming his way. Two Listeners came marching down the lane, a man and a woman. They were arguing in loud voices and luckily didn't notice the flash of a small red something as it bounded into the undergrowth.

Mr Puzzle's heart was racing. He decided to avoid the lane and make his way back to the hall hidden by the brambles and trees. When he was quite sure the Listeners had passed, he set off again. Ten seconds later the mobile phone in his pocket began to vibrate and ear-splitting music spilled out into the wood. Mr Puzzle immediately recognised the opening bars of Beethoven's Fifth Symphony. 'Ssssh!' he begged the phone. 'Not now!'

The Listeners had stopped. 'Did you hear that?' asked the man.

'It came from the wood,' said the woman. 'Over there!'

'Someone's spying on us,' said the man. He began to stride into the undergrowth.

Mr Puzzle's short arms couldn't reach the mobile in his pocket. He ran a short distance, then lay on his stomach and pressed his body on to the phone. On and on went Beethoven, *da,da,da*, *dumm*-ing, over and over again.

Have to get the coat off, thought Mr Puzzle. But how? Paws can't undo buttons. Frantically Mr Puzzle curled up and tore at the buttons with his sharp teeth. Off they came. Ping, ping, ping, ping. The weasel wriggled out of the red coat and bounded away from it as fast as he could.

'Found it!' called a voice behind him. 'Looks as if it belongs to some kid. It was in a baby's coat pocket.'

'Sorry, Mary Bright,' whispered Mr Puzzle.

CHAPTER TWELVE
The Alchemist

It was dark and Mr Puzzle had not returned. Gabriel and the two girls sat, disconsolately, on the edge of Sadie's bed. They had all given up making suggestions about what to do next. Mutara had brought them a delicious breakfast of porridge, eggs, bacon, toast and orange juice. Since then they had seen no one and eaten nothing. There had been a great deal of activity on the floors below, and they didn't dare to venture out of their dormitory.

Sadie half-heartedly swung her legs. 'To keep the blood flowing,' she said, 'otherwise they'll drop off. I think I'm going to die of inactivity.'

Lucy went one better. 'I'm going to die of thirst. That orange juice was hours and hours ago.'

Gabriel was worried about the weasel. 'Something's happened to Mr Puzzle,' he said gloomily. 'He wouldn't leave us in the dark, knowing our situation.'

'And it really is dark,' said Lucy.' 'She had turned

on the light as soon as evening clouds came rolling across the sky.

The noise below was increasing every minute. Bursts of raucous laughter echoed up the main staircase, and now there was music: a drum, a cello and a flute of some kind. A shrill soprano began to join the instruments in an eerie melody, and other, less tuneful, voices rumbled in behind her. The music swelled. Feet thumped on the slate floors, hands clapped in time to the beat.

Gabriel slid off the bed and went to the window. 'What's going on?' he said, staring down at the cars in the lamplit drive. Several figures moved in the shadows beyond the drive and, all at once, there was a shrill whistle. A brilliant white light shot into the air.

Sadie and Lucy ran to his side and were just in time to see a shower of sparks falling through the dark sky.

'Fireworks!' said Lucy. 'It must be a celebration of some kind.'

An unthinkable possibility occurred to Gabriel. 'She's found the cloak,' he said, almost under his breath.

'No, she hasn't,' said Sadie. 'It's New Year's Eve, that's all.'

Gabriel gave a sigh of relief. 'Of course. I didn't think the sorceress would go in for that sort of thing

– music, singing and fireworks.'

'But look!' Lucy pointed at the window. 'They're not happy fireworks.'

This was true. A thin blue light was tracing a bright line through the sky. It was drawing a portrait. A cruel face emerged, its grim features demanding attention. Tiny flames issued from the nose and the corners of the narrow eyes.

When the dreadful face disintegrated the children thought the display was done, but suddenly fiery skeletons appeared, and a monstrous creature reared its head. It looked like a horned dinosaur with a long nose, and it came so close to the windowpane they could have touched it.

Lucy drew back, tugging Sadie with her. 'I wish it would stop,' she said huskily. 'They're not proper fireworks at all.'

Gabriel agreed, but there was no escape from the awful show. They could turn their backs to the window, but they could still hear the whistling and shrieking of the pyrotechnic horrors, and they could still hear the painful music and wildly applauding guests.

Lucy suggested it might be a good time to visit Tom and his sisters. 'And I'm dying to go to the toilet,' she added.

The others thought that it was a good idea. They

hadn't dared to leave the room while so much had been going on in the hall, but now the upstairs corridors seemed to be much quieter. All the guests were involved in fireworks and partying.

They crept out of the dormitory and up the dangerous stairway to the silent sisters' apartment.

Tom was very happy to see them. He had spent the day trying to make sense of his sisters' sign language and had grown quite hoarse from asking so many questions. Yuna had brought them some of the party food for supper.

'Salmon sandwiches,' said Tom, 'and lots of pasties with funny stuff inside, and tarts with icing, and chocolate mousses and nutty things.'

Lucy noticed a plate of food, still untouched on the table. Smiling, Dinah held it out to her. Lucy took three pasties.

'It was too much for us,' Tom explained. 'Yuna said "party", so perhaps it's someone's birthday.

'It's New Year's Eve,' said Sadie, helping herself to three unidentifiable things in paper cases, while Gabriel took the last salmon sandwich.

'New Year's Eve? Is it really?' said Tom, and his three spellbound sisters all opened their mouths in a big 'Oh', but their eyes held even more sadness than before. This meant they had been silent prisoners for more than a week.

Sadie asked if they'd heard the music and the sisters nodded.

'Weird music,' said Tom. 'We didn't like it.'

'And fireworks,' said Lucy, 'on our side of the building.'

Tom's eyes lit up. 'Fireworks?'

'Horrible fireworks,' Sadie told him.

'Can I come and see them?' Tom begged.

'They've finished,' Gabriel said quickly.

Tom slumped on a chair. 'I wish we could get out,' he muttered.

'We'll find a way soon,' said Gabriel, trying to believe his own words.

Between them the three visitors quickly polished off the last bits of the party supper. They visited the bathroom, drank some water and thanked the sisters for the food.

All three girls came to the door to watch the others carefully descend the creaking, squeaking steps. Bursts of almost satanic laughter crescendoed from below, and the sisters backed away and closed the door.

Gabriel and the girls ran back to the dormitory, heedless of any noise their feet might make. It seemed obvious that every Listener was occupied in the merrymaking.

Gabriel stood inside the door, while the girls

flung themselves on their beds.

'We always have a party at home, on New Year's Eve,' Lucy said disconsolately.

The others said nothing. Sadie remembered parties when her mother was alive, Gabriel was always told his sisters were too young to stay up until midnight.

I'm not getting anywhere, thought Gabriel. The cloak is as distant as ever. Erebus drove me, the black hat brought me and the grey coat showed me. But where is the cloak?

The false Albert's words came into his head, 'The snow took it, a girl's voice . . .' But what did she say? And where did the snow take the cloak?

'I'll have to find the false Albert,' he muttered.

Sadie heard him. She grabbed his arm. 'You're not thinking of –'

'They're all so occupied, singing, dancing and probably drinking, it's the best chance I'll ever have.'

'But how will you find the laboratory?' Sadie said, frowning.

Lucy joined in. 'If they find you, imagine! No, I can't imagine, it's too awful.'

'Look,' said Gabriel calmly. 'I've already met two Listeners, and they accepted me as one of the servants. 'I'll carry a tray, or something, from the kitchen.'

'You can't go all the way down to the kitchen,' said Sadie.

'Luigi will help me. He must know the word "laboratory" by now.' Gabriel unfastened Sadie's fingers from his arm and went to the door. 'Wish me luck.'

The girls opened their mouths, but Gabriel slipped out before they could say anything more to stop him.

Johnny Bright was looking through the kitchen window, when he saw lights shooting into the sky. He slipped out into the garden to get a better look. The snow was melting and the ground was soft and slippery. It was quite dark but there was a lot going on in the sky. Fireworks were shooting up towards the stars – wheels of flame, fountains of colour, and then a whirling face, flames creeping from its eyes and nose. A fiery skeleton flew over Johnny's head, and then a monster with bloody claws.

The fireworks weren't fun anymore. Johnny ran indoors. His mother was pacing round the kitchen, something she often did these days. Hetty Bean was asleep in an armchair, while Florence sat at the kitchen table, trying to draw a dead moth.

'There are fireworks coming out of Ludgarth Hall,' said Johnny.

Florence pricked up her ears. 'Fireworks?'

Mrs Bright stopped pacing. 'The usual New Year's

Eve display,' she said.

'No.' Johnny vehemently shook his head. 'Not usual. Come and see!'

Mrs Bright and Florence followed him outside. They gazed up into the night sky and Florence screamed.

'What an awful sight!' cried Mrs Bright.

Florence ran indoors with her hands over her ears, as if not hearing the awfulness would help her to forget the horrors in the sky.

Safely inside the house, Mary Bright shook Hetty Bean awake. 'They're having a party up at Ludgarth, and there's just a chance the guards will be off duty for it. I'm coming with you if you go up there. I'll follow you in my car.'

Hetty Bean tossed back her hair and rubbed her eyes. She had already tried to get into the hall, but had been prevented by grim-faced, big-eared guards at every entrance. When she'd threatened to call the police, they had just laughed.

'I fell asleep,' said Hetty, pulling herself out of the chair. 'Yes, yes, Mary. We'll go. I'll keep on trying until . . . well, until the end.'

'The end of what?' asked Florence.

'Of me,' said Hetty.

Mary Bright darted about the kitchen, making fresh sandwiches. Johnny wrapped a cake in tinfoil, and Florence ran to get cartons of orange juice.

'I'll follow with Florence and Johnny,' said Mary.

Johnny punched the air and shouted, 'Yay!'

'Then if anything happens to you, Hetty,' Mary went on, 'I'll be there.'

'And we can rescue Lucy,' said Johnny, 'and maybe Tom and his sisters?'

'If only Lucy would phone me,' Mary complained. 'Why doesn't she use the phone we gave to that weasel?'

'Because something happened to him, probably,' said Johnny.

'Poor Mr Puzzle,' said Florence, with a sigh.

They filled Hetty's hamper, and then all four set off.

Hetty drove slowly up the wooded lane, with Mary Bright and her two children in the car behind. They turned off their lights just before they reached the lamplit drive, and then rolled quietly into a space behind the large parked cars.

Guards were still patrolling the five entrances. Hetty could see the glow of their cigarettes. Now and again they would meet each other between the entrances, have a quick chat, give nasty laughs and stride back to their chosen doorways.

Hetty decided to wait until midnight when, surely, the guards would go inside to celebrate the New Year.

Sure enough, a few minutes before midnight all the guards disappeared. Hetty jumped out of the Land Rover and ran over to Mary's car.

'I'm going now,' said Hetty, tapping on Mary's window.

Mary gave a thumbs-up sign. Her children were fast asleep on the seats behind her.

Looking carefully all around her, Hetty walked slowly towards the nearest entrance – a tall, rather grand door. It was locked.

'Of course,' said Hetty to herself. 'All the doors will be locked.' She thought that if she waited another hour or two, everyone in the hall would be asleep and she could try to get in through a window. It wouldn't be the first time Hetty Bean had climbed into a high window. It was one of her specialities. Mountaineering was a favourite hobby, second only to cooking. Somewhere behind the walls of that grim stone building were her precious charges, and she would find them.

When Gabriel finally reached the kitchen it was so full of steam he could hardly see his way to the stove. He hoped to find Luigi cooking there. Pans bubbled, meat sizzled and strange languages were yelled across his head. Waiters with empty trays darted in through a green baize door, while waitresses with trays of glasses shouted their way past him. At last he found Luigi, carefully placing nuts on a vast chocolate cake.

Gabriel tapped the big chef's arm and Luigi jumped, dropping a handful of nuts. He turned to Gabriel and bellowed something in Italian, in a very cross voice.

'Sorry,' said Gabriel, and then he thought of Mr Puzzle. 'Mr Puzzle?' he asked.

Luigi's features softened. He shrugged, spread his hands and shook his head.

'Oh dear,' said Gabriel.

'Oh dear,' Luigi repeated, with feeling.

They would have to do something about the weasel later, but right now, Gabriel had to find the laboratory. 'Laboratory?' he asked.

Luigi frowned.

'For Mr Puzzle,' Gabriel lied, hoping it might stir Luigi's interest.

'Laboratory?' Luigi sounded suspicious.

Gabriel nodded. 'Lab–or–a–to–ry,' he said, enunciating every syllable.

Luigi pointed to a door in a far corner. 'On, on, on,' he said. 'On to end. Laboratory.'

'Thanks.' Gabriel took an empty tray from the counter. 'Can I . . .?'

Luigi put up a commanding finger. 'Wait!' He went to the end of the counter, opened a drawer and pulled out several white aprons. One by one he held them out and shook his head. They all looked far too long for Gabriel, but at last Luigi selected an apron that wasn't quite as large as the others.

Gabriel allowed himself to be tied into the apron. A round white hat was fitted on to his head, and at last Luigi said, 'OK.'

The door in the corner led into a long passage. Gabriel set off. He passed several ordinary looking doors before he suddenly came to a long open window. He hadn't been prepared for a hatch.

'Ah, boy!' A blond woman with long black earrings pushed several empty glasses through the hatch. 'More champagne,' she demanded.

Gabriel gaped at her headdress: a tower of white foam topped with cherries. Beyond the woman he could see masked figures dressed in cloaks. Some, like the blonde, wore extraordinary concoctions on their heads. Long feathers sprouted from sparkling headbands, spoons rattled on black helmets, white ribbons floated from judges' wigs and there was even a man with a pig's head perched above his own rather pig-like face.

Gabriel stood there a moment, gazing at the partygoers in horrified fascination.

'Shoo!' said the woman. 'Go on! CHAMPAGNE!'
Gabriel put the glasses on his tray and turned

back to the kitchen. When he got there, he dumped the glasses on a table, calling, 'Champagne,' to the nearest waiter, and set off again.

He could hardly believe his bad luck when, passing the hatch a second time, a white-haired man called, 'Boy, more wine,' and held up a tray of empty glasses.

Gabriel grimaced and took the tray. This time he caught a glimpse of a long table laden with food and drink. The band had been replaced by rather spine-chilling recorded music. He didn't linger, but sped back to the kitchen, as fast as he could without dropping the glasses. Once again, he dumped the tray on a table and called, 'Wine,' to the nearest waitress, who happened to be Yuna. She gave him a big wink and held up her thumb.

Gabriel grinned and rushed away. Hoping to avoid more demands he crawled beneath the hatch when he reached it. Before he could get to his feet, however, a door opened on the other side of the passage and a man stepped out. He wore a purple tricorn hat, and a black velvet jacket. 'What on earth are you doing?' he asked gruffly.

Gabriel looked up at the surly face. 'Mouse,' he said. 'See mouse.'

'Idiot,' said the man. He strode across the passage and entered the dining hall by a door next to the hatch.

Gabriel stood up. He began to run. If anyone stopped him, he decided to repeat the word 'mouse', whether they believed him or not.

He became aware that he was passing classrooms. A bronze plaque engraved with the name of a subject hung on almost every door. Bio-Drawing, whatever that was, Black Maths – Gabriel shuddered. Ex-Histories, Island Sorcery, Choral Fantasy.

Who would want to send their child to such a school? Gabriel wondered. At the very end of the passage he came to a door pitted with scorch marks. Set in the top half of the door was a pane of thick, bottle-green, wavy glass. Above the pane the word *Laboratory* had been painted in uneven black strokes.

Gabriel peered through the glass. He could see a figure moving slowly behind a long table. Bottles of every size and colour stood on the table, blue flames flickered beneath a copper saucepan on a trivet, and a powdery substance rose from a wide metal bowl.

Gabriel took a deep breath and opened the door. The man behind the table stood directly opposite him. He stared at Gabriel with cold blue eyes. His hands were bandaged and yellowing bruises covered his face. There was nothing recognisable about the man, except for his eyes.

'Good evening, Gabriel Silk!' The man spoke

through swollen lips. His speech was slurred, and yet there was something familiar in his tone.

They stood unmoving for a moment, staring at each other.

'I know you,' said Gabriel. And yet, *did* he know this person? This thin, bald man? Gone were the thick white hair, the big moustache, the whiskery eyebrows. This man was completely hairless. 'You're the false Albert Blackstaff,' he said.

'Briefly,' the man agreed. 'In a wig and a false moustache and a bit of padding. My name is Amos Arkright.'

'You stole the king's cloak,' said Gabriel.

Amos sniffed sadly. 'I stole the cloak, and now I'm being punished for losing it.'

'I know that,' said Gabriel. 'I wore your hat, and your coat.'

'Did you now? You're the boy who lives through other people's clothes, aren't you?'

Amos seemed to be mocking him. 'I don't *live* through others' clothes,' Gabriel objected, 'I've got a life of my own. But I saw your mangled coat in a room upstairs, so I put it on, and it took me back to the day when you stole the cloak. There was a voice in the snow, a girl's voice. I'm trying to find out where the cloak went. Perhaps, when I was in your coat, I missed something. Perhaps I didn't hear everything the voice was trying to say. I thought you could help, that's why I'm here.'

Amos gave a strangled laugh. 'Don't you think I want to know, too? Don't you think I've been wondering and trying to remember and torturing myself with doubt? I wish I'd never heard of that wretched cloak, never sent that invitation to your father.'

'Then why did you?'

Amos looked away. 'They promised me more than I could ever dream of. And I believed them.'

Gabriel shook his head. What a fool the man was!

'Yes, I'm an idiot,' Amos said gloomily. 'I never stopped to think what those awful Forks would do to Albert Blackstaff.'

'And the false cloak?' asked Gabriel. 'Where did that come from?'

'Cecily made it. She said it was an exact replica of the real one. She'd seen a picture of it, many years ago, and then she got people researching it to make sure nothing could go wrong.' Amos paused and licked his swollen lips. 'More than anything I regret what happened to those girls. I never dreamt Cecily could be so cruel.'

'What girls?' Gabriel suddenly thought of Tom's sisters.

Amos shuffled up and down behind his table, touching jars, picking up pieces of chalk in his bandaged fingers and tapping them on the table. He extinguished the blue flames and peered into the copper saucepan.

'What girls?' Gabriel demanded.

Amos stared ahead, avoiding Gabriel's eye. 'I was in the ante-rom, beside the hall, trying on the wigs Loth gave me, strapping a cushion across my stomach. The carol singers were arriving. I had to hurry. And then the door opened and there were these girls, staring in. My wig was all askew. I yelled at them, and off they went, but not before . . . well . . .' He heaved a sigh.

'Not before what?' pressed Gabriel.

Amos regarded his bandaged hands. 'They saw the false cloak,' he murmured. 'It was lying over the back of a chair, a beautiful, sparkling red cloak. Those Touchstone girls just gazed at it, their eyes wide with wonder. They would have talked about it, no doubt about that.'

'You told the sorceress,' Gabriel accused him.

'She couldn't afford to let them go. You know how news spreads from town to town, and all these ways of spreading gossip on the Internet.'

Gabriel gripped the table. 'What did the sorceress do?'

'Ugh!' Amos turned away. 'She shrieked and pointed at their mouths. They couldn't move, didn't make a sound, just . . . dropped to the ground. "You'll never leave this place alive," she told them. She was in a kind of frenzy.'

Gabriel felt sick. He couldn't think what to say.

'I'm just an alchemist,' muttered Amos. 'I teach the students, that's all. I didn't expect . . .' He shrugged. 'I truly regret . . . she can never let those girls out, or me, because I have seen –'

There were light footsteps in the passage. Gabriel quickly crawled under the table and moved to the far end, away from the door. He wondered if Amos would betray him.

'Hello, silly Amos!' said a high voice.

'What do you want, Septimus?' said Amos, guardedly.

'I want to play with your mercury; all those little silver balls, rolling up and down in their glass tubes.'

'Mercury is dangerous,' said Amos.

'I don't care,' Septimus said with a snort. 'I don't like the party any more. The relatives are weird.'

'Surely they're not all relatives,' said Amos.

'Yes, they are. They come from that place where Mother was born. Endov. They're big-eared and mean and not fun, and now they are stupid with wine. If you don't give me any mercury I'll get them to punish you.'

'One more blow would hardly matter,' grunted

Amos. 'You're not having any mercury.'

'We'll see about that,' yelled Septimus. 'Don't think I haven't seen that *person* under your table.' He rushed out, slamming the door so hard, the green glass window rattled in its frame.

Amos looked under the table. 'You'd better get out of here,' he told Gabriel, 'as fast as you can.'

CHAPTER THIRTEEN
A Party Turns Bad

Gabriel crawled out from under the table, ran to the door and opened it carefully.

'Thanks,' he said to Amos, and leapt into the passage.

There was only one way to go, he thought, back the way he had come. But, just as he was about to make a dash for the kitchen, he noticed a narrow recess beside the laboratory door. He peeped in.

A set of steep steps led up into the darkness. They looked inviting. Why? Gabriel wasn't at all sure. But he found himself mounting the dark steps two at a time. He hadn't stopped to think where he might find himself. The steps were so narrow he thought they would lead to some shadowy attic where he could hide for a while.

Septimus was bound to report what he had seen. But what *had* he seen? A foot? Two feet? They could have belonged to anyone. Gabriel began to relax.

The sorceress had no idea that he was here, or that Sadie, Lucy and Tom were in the house. He continued to climb.

The steps twisted and turned several times before reaching a velvet curtain. Pushing it aside, Gabriel found himself on a balcony above the great hall. He could see the chain of the chandelier hanging from a large stucco flower on the ceiling and, leaning over the balcony rail, he looked down on groups of people moving unsteadily through the crowded room. The candles in the chandelier had all been extinguished, and flickering oil-lamps were the only source of light. The music was gloomy and repetitive, but the guests sang lustily, the words reaching Gabriel in a droning sort of hum.

They're out of their minds, he thought. He began to walk slowly along the balcony, hoping to see another staircase leading off it. The only lamp, in a bracket, halfway down, was very dim and it was difficult to see anything in the gloom. When a large hand came down on his shoulder he almost choked with fright.

'Got you!' said an oily voice, and Gabriel was tugged round to face his assailant.

He looked up into Ichabod Loth's overlarge, sludge-green eyes.

'Good evening, intruder!' The doctor's voice oozed like fat in a drain.

Gabriel thought he might faint. Mustn't do that, he told himself. Keep cool, Gabriel. He doesn't know who you are.

But Septimus's moon-face peered round Dr Loth's elbow. 'That's Sadie Silk's cousin!' he cried. 'The weird one with a seventh sense. She's got a photo of him. See, I was right to tell you about the foot I saw, wasn't I, Dad-to-be?'

Gabriel was almost sure that Ichabod winced.

'You were quite right, Septimus,' said Dr Loth.

'And it's a good thing you didn't drink as much of that awful stuff as Mum and the relatives.'

'A very good thing,' agreed Septimus's dad-to-be. 'So what am I going to do with you, Gabriel Silk, Keeper of the Cloak?'

Gabriel shrugged. 'It's pretty obvious I haven't got the cloak, or I wouldn't be here, would I?'

'I said, WHAT AM I GOING TO DO WITH YOU?' Dr Loth's voice became loud and heavy.

'I suppose you could just let me go,' said Gabriel. 'I haven't done any harm.'

'You have trespassed,' said Ichabod Loth. 'You're an intruder, a thief, a violent thug in need of punishments.'

Gabriel swallowed. 'Punishments?' he said weakly.

The doctor's laugh was even worse than his speaking voice. It gurgled like a swamp. 'That's right, PUNISHMENTS!'

When Septimus joined in with his spiteful giggling, Gabriel decided he'd had enough. Whisking round, he made a dash for the curtain he could see beneath the wall lamp.

There were indeed steps behind the curtain or, to be more precise, a stepladder, but it ascended instead of descending as Gabriel had hoped. There was no time to hesitate. He began to climb.

'You're going for the roof, are you?' said Dr Loth, close behind. 'Not much hope there, boy, unless you can fly.'

Gabriel gritted his teeth. He had no idea what he would do when he reached the roof. Perhaps he would see a drainpipe or a chimney, anything would do. But his hopes came to nothing when he felt a long arm twine itself around his legs.

It was not a normal arm. It grew. It lengthened and became a rope, a thick, sinewy snake of a rope. The squeezing arm tugged and Gabriel clung to the wooden step above him until he thought his arms would come out of their sockets. His fingers began to lose their grip and he knew that it was only a matter of time before he let go.

Just as Gabriel was about to give up a thin beam of light appeared above his head. The beam widened as a trap door was lifted, revealing a sparkling green mist.

There was an astonished gasp from Dr Loth and the long arm round Gabriel's legs began to slacken.

Septimus squeaked, 'What's that?'

Gabriel's whole body began to relax. 'Etzel,' he breathed.

The mist moved closer and Etzel's slight frame appeared, surrounded by the floating winged creatures. The scent of spices was more intense than ever.

Septimus gave a howl of shock and he thudded to the floor. Dr Loth groaned and growled. His extraordinarily long arm seemed to wither and Gabriel was free.

There was a moan of helpless fury as the doctor slithered off the steps and crashed to the floor.

For a moment, Gabriel felt too chilled by the sounds to move. But Etzel continued to descend. The phantom had no need to climb backwards, but appeared to drift slowly down the ladder, his large, shining eyes holding Gabriel's gaze as he began to step back.

Stepping over the groaning doctor and whimpering boy, Gabriel reached the balcony. Etzel was immediately at his side. The phantom leaned over the two bodies and murmured, 'Too many hinder thee, O Keeper, they must be slowed.' His elegant right hand made a sweeping motion over Septimus and the doctor, and they fell silent.

Gabriel could hardly bring himself to look at them, but when he did their open mouths and wide staring eyes made him feel quite ill. 'What have you done to them?' he whispered.

Etzel smiled. 'Quietened,' he said, 'for a day or two,' and then he took his mist along the balcony, and Gabriel followed, looking back, just once, at the motionless huddle of the boy and his dad-to-be.

No one else will know, he thought, and no one does know that I am here. For some reason he didn't believe that Amos would give him away.

Leaving the balcony Etzel drifted down the stairwell, while Gabriel, keeping in the shelter of the phantom mist, climbed down behind him.

On reaching the laboratory door, Gabriel looked in on the alchemist. Amos was putting bottles in a glass cabinet. He looked round and saw a boy in a white apron with a green mist floating around him. Amos almost dropped a bottle.

'You should leave here, Amos,' said Gabriel.

'Wha . . .' Amos began.

'You should go while you can.'

'Where would I go?' said Amos, 'And what's that mist behind you?'

'I can't explain,' said Gabriel. 'But you're an alchemist. I'm sure you would be valuable anywhere. Now's the time to leave, while the party's still going on.'

Gabriel felt a hand on his shoulder.

'Do not tarry,' said Etzel, and he drifted away.

Amos clapped a hand over his eyes. 'I'm not seeing right,' he grunted.

'Goodbye, Amos,' said Gabriel.

He hurried after the phantom, forgetting to drop to his knees when he passed the hatch. But he need not have bothered. The guests appeared to have forgotten all about it. They were gliding across the floor, waving their arms and singing in some of the worst voices that Gabriel had ever heard.

Etzel was fast approaching the kitchen door. If the staff saw a green phantom, horrible accidents could occur, probably involving broken crockery and scalding sauces.

'Wait! Wait!' hissed Gabriel. 'You mustn't go in there.'

Etzel half-turned and the green mist shifted a little. 'Thou must not tarry,' he said.

'Don't go into the kitchen,' warned Gabriel.

"'Tis the way.'

'But not for you, Etzel. You didn't come that way before, did you? How did you get to the roof?'

The phantom gave a whimsical smile. 'For me 'twas yet another waking place.'

'Please don't go in there.' Gabriel pointed at the kitchen door. 'They're very busy, and you might cause an accident.'

'Tush,' said Etzel with a sniff. 'We must be gone. Thou hast lingered here too long. I will await thee at the entrance.'

Gabriel realised that Etzel's extraordinary power could probably overcome the guards, if any still remained outside. 'I can't come yet,' he told the phantom. 'I must fetch my friends.'

'What is this nonsense?' Etzel was beginning to sound severe. 'Thou art the Keeper, thou must search. Erebus demands it.'

'Erebus? He's here?' said Gabriel, in dismay.

"'Tis unwise to anger him.'

'But my friends,' Gabriel said desperately, 'and the silent sisters, I can't leave without them.'

Etzel's attitude changed completely. 'True,' he said softly, 'sisters must be saved, and sorcery undone.'

'Yes,' Gabriel said firmly. 'So thou must await us at the entrance, and, somehow, I'll find a way to reach you with my friends.'

Etzel gazed over Gabriel's head. 'My sister's hair was autumn brown,' he murmured, 'it curled like ivy leaves, and her cheeks had kisses from the sun.'

It might have worked out just as Gabriel hoped, if there hadn't been an ear-splitting scream from the kitchen.

Etzel swung round and stared at the door. Gabriel hesitated, and then he heard Luigi roar, 'Fantasma! Aaah!'

'Erebus,' said Gabriel.

Etzel spread his hands, looking anxious.

Gabriel entered the kitchen and the green phantom followed.

Luigi was standing by the stove, a heavy frying pan held aloft, while Erebus growled his way around the long kitchen counter. 'Cloak,' he snarled. 'Where is't? Not here methinks.'

The rest of the kitchen staff were huddled by the back wall. Some were sobbing, one of them had fainted. When Etzel appeared, another one dropped to the floor. But Luigi wasn't daunted. He could take on two phantoms if he had to.

'Go!' he roared. 'Vai vai!'

Erebus saw Gabriel and hissed, 'Keeper, do not tarry here. Do thy duty!' He pointed to the exit.

'Not . . . yet . . .' Gabriel put his hand over his nose as the phantom came close, his stench overpowering.

'This instant, or death will be thy fate!' Out came his long nail on its bony finger. But, all at once, Etzel stepped in front of Gabriel and swung the claw away.

'The Keeper hath first another task,' said Etzel. 'A moment to save friends.'

'And I must drive, drive, drive the Keeper to his duty,' snarled Erebus.

'And where lies the king's cloak?' asked Etzel.

'It is not for me to know,' retorted Erebus. ''Tis the Keeper's task to search.'

'Patience, Erebus,' demanded Etzel.

'None to spare,' screeched Erebus, thrusting his fist into Etzel's stomach. 'Thou art a traitor, Etzel, Count of Orestone. Likewise thy sister.'

Bent double with pain, Etzel charged at Erebus who staggered back, then kicked the green phantom's legs. Etzel's frail body gave way and he sank to his knees. Erebus stepped round him, reaching for Gabriel, who found that he couldn't move. Was it fear, or was it the power of the oldest, meanest Sleeper?

Gabriel stood helpless as the skeletal fingers stretched towards his arm. One moment the phantom was staring into his face, the next he was falling on to the floor, his grey shroud folding over him. Etzel had grabbed his ankles and tugged.

As soon as Erebus fell, Etzel was up. He drifted

swiftly towards the door into the great hall, while Gabriel, in a weak voice, begged him not to. Suddenly Erebus reared up and flew after the green phantom. Etzel opened the door and both phantoms were gone.

It was the moment when Gabriel should have run to fetch his friends, while the sorceress and her guests were distracted by the phantom Sleepers. But, hardly aware of what he was doing, Gabriel followed the phantoms. He feared for Etzel and had to know what happened to him.

As Gabriel entered the great hall, still in the cap and apron Luigi had put on him, he was astonished to hear applause. The guests had moved back to watch the phantoms tussle. First Etzel would fall, then Erebus; their thin arms flailed, their bones creaked and their grey shrouds swirled and fluttered.

'Marvellous,' called a man whose mouth sounded as if it were full of marshmallows. 'Great conjuring!'

A woman slumped in a chair shrilled, 'Your betrothed promised us a spectacle, Cecily. This is excellent!'

'Love the green mist!' Gabriel recognised the blond woman who had demanded champagne. She looked as if she'd been dragged through a bush, with mascara on her cheeks, lipstick on her chin and hair all awry. 'Where is the good doctor, Cecily?' she asked.

'He's pulling strings behind the scenes,' said a

213

husky voice.

Gabriel searched the room for the sorceress, and there she was, reclining on a velvet couch. Her knife-like hair had lost its shine, her dress was crumpled and her pale face rouged like a clown's.

'Is this the spectacle Ichabod promised?' asked another guest.

The sorceress smiled. 'It seems that my Ichabod can summon spirits at will. He has kept this secret, even from me.'

Her smile faded as Erebus pushed his way through the guests, grabbing for Etzel. People began to hold their noses and back away from the awful stench that wafted out from him. Someone said, 'This isn't such fun. The smell will kill us.'

Etzel whirled into an empty space, his shroud billowing like a cloud, and then he vanished.

Erebus turned and turned, snarling, his claw-like nails stabbing at everyone within his reach. The guests that were still on their feet began to hurl whatever they could find. Glass bowls, silver candlesticks, brass trays, jugs, china, bottles all came flying at the phantom. They bounced off his bony head like rubber and crashed on to the floor, the glass shattering into a thousand pieces.

Now, the crunch of glass shards punctuated the roars of fear as the infuriated Erebus tore into the crowd, his fatal fingers sweeping over their faces and transfixing them, until every guest was silent and immobile. As soon as the moans and groans had died away, Erebus began to fade.

Gabriel ran from the silent room. 'Gone! Fantasma gone!' he told Luigi.

'Gone?' said Luigi, lowering his heavy pan.

'And the guests are . . . well, asleep.'

Some of the other staff moved closer, staring at Gabriel. Several of them murmured, 'Gone?' They cupped their hands to their ears and listened. No sound came from the party-goers. Gabriel wished he could explain things a little better. If only Mr Puzzle were with them. Where *was* Mr Puzzle?

'Sorry,' Gabriel said lamely, as he made for the stairway.

Yuna grinned and waved him on.

Away from the kitchen, the house was very quiet. Gabriel bounded up to the dormitory, opened the door and sang out 'Happy New Year!'

He was greeted with silence. Well, not quite silence – the girls were breathing heavily.

'Wake up,' said Gabriel, turning on the light.

Sadie rolled over, saying, 'Wh . . . a . . . a . . . t?' in a sleepy voice.

'Happy New Year!' said Gabriel, bouncing on to her bed.

'Go to sleep,' said Sadie.

Gabriel tugged her bedclothes. 'All the guests are out of it. The phantom Sleepers have done their worst. Mind you, everyone was pretty far gone before the phantoms got there. Come on, we've got to go now.'

CHAPTER FOURTEEN
A Castle in Flames

Lucy was now wide awake. 'They'll catch us before we get out, I know they will,' she whined.

Gabriel shook his head. 'The phantoms have done for them,' he said confidently. 'Most of them, anyway. Dr Loth and Septimus are at the top of the house, spellbound, or worse. But the cloak's not here, and I've got to go on searching.'

'What about the sorceress?' asked Lucy.

Gabriel had to admit that he wasn't sure about the sorceress. They would just have to take their chances.

The girls rubbed their eyes, shook out their hair and put on their shoes and coats.

'We must take Tom and his sisters,' said Sadie.

'Of course.' Gabriel couldn't untangle himself from the apron, so he flung on his anorak and all three ran out of the door.

When they reached the creaking steps Gabriel climbed up to the apartment where Tom's sisters had been imprisoned. Sadie and Lucy waited below.

The door was unlocked and he crept inside.

In a small chamber beyond the living room, Gabriel found the three girls asleep on narrow truckle beds. A lantern burned on a small table in the corner.

He went to Dinah's bed first and gently touched her shoulder. 'Dinah! Dinah, wake up!' he whispered.

Her eyes opened and she stared at him fearfully.

'We can leave this place,' he said. 'There's no one to stop us.'

Dinah pulled the bedclothes up to her chin. She wouldn't move.

Gabriel went to Poppy's bed next. He woke her with a light prod and repeated his message. 'We can leave here. There's no one about.'

Poppy frowned, she shook her head and turned away from him.

By the time Gabriel reached Leonora she was already awake. Tom rolled out from under her bed and stood up, crying, 'We can go, all of us, really?'

'They're all sort of asleep,' Gabriel told him. He went to the door. 'We must go now, before it's too late. Put on your coats. It's cold outside.'

The three girls hadn't moved. They shook their heads, perhaps afraid of being caught by yet another spell.

'Come on! Come on!' begged Tom. 'Let's go.

Dinah, Poppy, Leonora, please get up!'

One by one they slowly threw back their covers and swung their legs off the beds. They were all wearing long, white nightgowns with lace collars covering their necks, and frills around their wrists – garments left by the reclusive aunt.

Gabriel went into the living room and waited. He opened the door and looked down on to Sadie's anxious face. 'They're coming,' he said. But were they?

Eventually Tom led his sisters out of the bedroom. They had no coats and still wore their white, Victorian nightdresses. All they had on their feet were thin slippers.

'I think their coats and shoes were taken,' said Tom.

Gabriel shrugged. 'Never mind. We'll worry about coats when we're out. Come on!' He began to descend the ancient steps. Tom was already following him.

When both boys were at the bottom, they looked up to see the girls frozen in the doorway. Tom begged them to move quickly. They shook their heads. Gabriel called to them, Sadie and Lucy added their voices, nervously, desperately – they were afraid to wait much longer.

Leonora put out her foot and placed it on the top step. Immediately, she fell back into her sisters' arms.

'They're not afraid of being caught,' Gabriel said, under his breath. 'They can't leave the room.'

Tom scrambled up to his sisters, begging them to try again. But Leonora lay on the floor, gasping for breath, her eyes wide, her hands fluttering beside her head like frantic birds.

'It's the same curse,' Sadie said quietly. 'Like Dad, they can't leave, or they will die.'

'No, no, no,' sobbed Tom.

Tears streamed down Poppy's cheeks, Dinah stroked her hair and looked at Gabriel, shaking her head once again.

'I'm not leaving them,' said Tom. He crawled through the doorway and sat beside Leonora.

Dinah gave a brief little wave and closed the door.

The others stood helplessly at the bottom step, appalled by the cruel spell.

'There's nothing more we can do,' Gabriel said at last.

They crept uneasily down the next staircase. Gabriel couldn't get the silent sisters' desolate faces out of his head. I will come back, he promised himself, when I have the cloak.

The kitchen appeared to be deserted, and then they saw Luigi, sitting on a stool at the end of the long counter. 'All gone!' he said, smiling.

'Gone?' said Gabriel, 'Yuna, Mutara, all of them?'

'All,' said Luigi. 'I go soon.'

Suddenly a small head popped up in front of Luigi.

'Hello, children,' said Mr Puzzle. 'Happy New Year!'

'Mr Puzzle!' cried all three children. They rushed to the weasel, patting his head, stroking his back and generally making a big fuss of him.

'Where've you been?' Sadie demanded. 'We were so worried.'

'Long story,' said the weasel. 'I was tangled in a teddy's coat. Then when I got here, I couldn't get in, could I? Those wretched guards were watching all the entrances like hawks.'

'So how did you get past them?' asked Gabriel.

'They went inside, couldn't miss seeing in the New Year, could they? Of course they shut all the doors, but just now Yuna, Mutara and the others all rushed out, nearly knocked me over. "Where are you going?" I said, and Mutara replied, "Anywhere. We have to go. It's bad, bad inside." Then they got into one of those big cars and Yuna drove them off. She's very good with things like that, starting cars and stuff.'

Sadie uttered a loud, 'Phew!'

'The guards must have joined the other guests,' said Gabriel, 'and they're all . . . sort of . . . frozen, you could say. So, let's go!' Gabriel went to the door to the outside passage.

'Come on, Luigi,' said Sadie. 'Come with us!'

'OK!' Luigi agreed.

Gabriel held the door open while Luigi strode towards him, holding Sadie's hand. But just before they reached the door, a rasping voice shrieked, 'You haven't a chance, vermin!'

Gabriel's hand slipped from the door and it slammed shut behind him. Lucy covered her eyes with her hands, while Sadie put one hand over her obsidian star. Luigi stepped protectively in front of everyone.

Cecily Fork stood at the other end of the counter. The stiff strands of her hair were dull, her skintight sequinned dress sagged, its neckline torn. She looked too worn for any spells, but her pale eyes blazed with sorcery. 'You came for the cloak, foolish Gabriel Silk, but you haven't got it, have you?'

Gabriel took a breath and stepped out from behind Luigi. He found that his anger eclipsed his fear of the sorceress. She had no heart, her false cloak had told him that. 'I don't have it yet, Cecily Fork, but I will have it, very soon,' he said defiantly.

'And how's that? Do you think your aged phantoms will help you?' She gave a snort of derision. 'Perhaps the stinking one can drain our strength for a while, but his power will not last, my people are beginning to wake already. And as for that pathetic green ghost, he wouldn't know how to help you.'

Sadie leapt in front of Gabriel. 'He's not pathetic,'

she cried. 'He came from the Red King, and he's noble and brave.'

The sorceress threw back her head and gave such a raucous shriek of mirth it made Sadie shake with fury. But she took a step towards the sorceress and said, in a low voice, 'One day you will be punished, Cecily Fork.'

'Stupid girl, you were always a thorn in my side,' snarled the sorceress, lifting her dangerous hands. 'You're vermin, both of you.'

The children stood their ground, almost expecting whiskers to grow on their cheeks, or fur to cover their hands, but all at once the sorceress gave a deafening screech and fell to the ground.

Gabriel reached for the door behind him, pulled it open and shouted, 'Run!'

All three children, followed by Luigi, dashed through.

Something brushed Sadie's leg as she ran. Looking down, she saw Mr Puzzle grinning up at her. There was blood on his nose and chin.

'Ankle,' he said.

Sadie, light-headed with relief, began to giggle. 'Mr Puzzle bit Cecily's ankle,' she said happily.

'Both ankles,' said the weasel.

They weren't out of danger yet, but a wild elation overcame them, and they all began to laugh.

'Hooray for Mr Puzzle,' sang Lucy.

'Hooray!' Luigi agreed.

They burst out of the last door, and then they were in the cold air of the car park. They rushed down the lamplit avenue towards the trees, Luigi panting heavily behind them. They were almost at the end of the drive when a familiar voice shouted at them to stop.

'Gabriel! Sadie!' Hetty Bean came running towards them.

Mary Bright wasn't far behind her, with Florence and Johnny in tow. 'Lucy! Lucy!' shouted all three Brights.

Before they knew it the children were being kissed, clasped and hugged.

'This is Luigi,' said Gabriel, coming up for air, so Hetty included Luigi in her embrace, and he happily returned it.

'Oh, a chef,' cried Hetty ecstatically, taking in the white hat still perched firmly on Luigi's head.

'Very appropriate,' Mr Puzzle remarked, as he tried to avoid the stampede.

'We'd better go,' said Gabriel. 'Cecily Fork is still about.'

'Into the car, children!' Mary Bright hurried her three into the car, promising to ring Hetty later. She drove away while her children's hands waved from every window.

Sadie and Gabriel jumped into the back of the Land Rover, and Luigi hauled himself up beside Hetty. Mr Puzzle leapt on to the chef's lap at the last moment.

As they sped past the rows of black cars, Sadie couldn't resist looking back, just to make sure the sorceress wasn't following.

Cecily Fork stood in the open doorway. She was pointing at the Land Rover, her lips moving endlessly, as though she were chanting a poem she'd learnt by heart.

'She's there!' Sadie grabbed Gabriel's arm. 'I think she's sending a spell.'

Gabriel turned and saw the sorceress. A line of flames suddenly erupted from the ground before her. They streaked across the drive towards the Land Rover.

'She's trying to burn us!' he cried. 'Hetty, can you go faster?'

'I'll do my best,' she said.

The car leapt forward, bouncing them in their seats, and they watched a single flame darting after them, but never quite catching up.

The Land Rover began to bump down the wooded hill, and the sorceress vanished from view. Soon they had even lost sight of the great grey hall, and Sadie muttered, 'It'll take her a while to recover from *that* spell.'

When they reached the end of the lane, Hetty turned on to the road that led away from Ludgarth, and Luigi suddenly said, 'Train, please.'

'Of course, but must we lose you so soon?' said Hetty.

Luigi answered with a stream of Italian that Mr Puzzle interpreted at intervals. 'He says, for now, he must go . . . to his brother in London . . . he always keeps his money and papers with him . . . so no trouble there . . . and he . . . he . . . will be in touch again, very soon.'

'Wonderful,' said Hetty. She made a slight detour to another town, where they dropped Luigi at the train station.

It was very early and a train to London was not expected for several hours, but Luigi was happy to wait. So, with more hugs and promises of meetings to come, they said goodbye. Hetty seemed a little nervous about leaving him alone, but Mr Puzzle assured her that Luigi could take care of himself.

Soon they were out on the empty moor, where the sky was still dotted with stars, and a pale moon floated above invisible hills.

'Tuck in to the hamper,' Hetty told the children, 'and when you've had your breakfast, you'd better take a nap. It's a long drive.'

'What about you, Hetty?' asked Sadie. 'You'll need someone to talk to, to keep awake.'

'I've got Mr Puzzle,' said Hetty. 'I can't wait to hear about some of his adventures.'

'There have indeed been many,' said Mr Puzzle, who had to grip the seat belt with his teeth, whenever Hetty changed gear, 'but none,' he added, 'have been quite as unusual as this.'

'You probably saved our lives, Mr Puzzle,' said Sadie, popping a sandwich on to his seat. 'This will taste better than the blood of a sorceress.'

While they tucked in to the food, Gabriel told them what had happened to Dr Loth and Septimus.

'Septimus had it coming to him,' Sadie said with satisfaction.

'Oh, I nearly forgot,' said Gabriel, munching on a chocolate brownie. 'The phantoms had a fight before Erebus started sending people into trances. And Etzel is a count.'

Sadie gave a sigh of wonder. 'A count. He really looks like one, doesn't he?'

'I wouldn't know,' said Gabriel, 'but Erebus called him Count of Orestone.' Suddenly an image came into his mind. He saw Etzel opening a door and looking in at the silent sisters.

'We couldn't rescue the Touchstone sisters,' he told Mr Puzzle. 'I feel I should have tried harder.

Tom wouldn't leave them, so, in a way, he's now just as trapped as they are.'

'We'll get them out.' Mr Puzzle sounded very confident. 'There'll be a way.'

This made the children feel a little better, but then there was the question of the spell. How would that be lifted? This was on all their minds, but none of them could bring themselves to say it out loud. Gabriel felt that Mr Puzzle might be relying on him for a solution.

The cloak, he thought, it will solve everything – if we can find it.

The hamper was soon empty and, one by one, the children fell asleep. But not for long. They were woken up by a loud exclamation from Hetty, and a lot of excited chatter from Mr Puzzle.

'What's happened?' said Gabriel, half-expecting to see the sorceress glaring in at them.

'Flat tyre,' said Hetty. 'I think a flame must have reached the wheel. It's probably been slowly deflating and now it's worn right through.' She pulled over, got out and began to pull a new tyre from the boot.

Gabriel jumped out, ready to help, but Hetty said she'd been driving tractors since she was twelve and could change a wheel on her own anytime. Gabriel could see now that the back wheel had been burned quite badly. It looked black and shiny, and they were lucky it hadn't stopped them before.

Once the wheel was changed, they set off again. This time they stayed awake, watching the moon disappear and the stars gradually fade.

By mid-morning they were driving down Meldon High Street. The shops were still bright with Christmas decorations, but many were closed. It was New Year's Day. The packed snow beside the road was beginning to thaw, and the sun was out.

Melting snow trickled down the roof of The Carpenter's Cabin. It filled the gutters and dripped on to the soggy garden.

Sadie ran up the path and rang the bell insistently. When it was finally opened she flew into her father's arms, babbling about the sorceress, the phantom Sleepers and the silent sisters. 'But, Dad, the cloak wasn't there,' she said, wildly shaking her head.

'Come and tell Paton.' Jack Silk led everyone into the kitchen.

Paton Yewbeam didn't appear to have stirred since the children had left. He was still sitting in the same chair, with one of the enormous books open before him. In fact, all the other books had been brought back into the kitchen, where they covered the table, just as before. Paton didn't seem too disheartened by Sadie's news, but gave a resigned smile and patted his books.

The only thing that had changed in the kitchen was the pile of dirty crockery, which filled the sink and now threatened to overflow onto the draining board.

'Honestly, Dad. You could have washed up,' Sadie remarked with a wry smile.

'We've been very busy,' said Jack, looking bashful. 'But you'll be glad to hear that your parents are back, Gabriel. I still haven't told them about the cloak. I felt I should but . . .'

'Not yet,' said Paton. 'They're worried about Albert, and there's still a chance to find the cloak.'

Gabriel felt a cold wave of dread when he heard those words. 'Just a chance? There must be more than a chance,' he cried. 'I have to find the cloak, because . . . because . . .'

Four anxious faces were staring at him.

'It's not what you think,' said Gabriel. 'I'm not scared of what Erebus can do – it's just that I realise how much I miss the cloak. I don't think I can exist without it . . . without going to the attic when I'm sad, and putting it round my shoulders and . . . and feeling better. I was the Keeper when it was lost and so *I* have to find it.'

'Of course,' said Paton, 'and somehow the cloak *will* be found. We must just put our heads together.'

There was a profound silence, and then Sadie said,

'Was the real Albert badly injured?'

'He's out of hospital,' said her father, 'but shocked, of course. The perpetrator can't be found.'

Gabriel told them about Amos, but after hearing of his fate, Uncle Jack and Paton agreed that the poor man had been foolish rather than wicked, and had probably suffered enough.

Tea and hot chocolate were made. Paton's precious books were cleared away and replaced by a large plate of scones. While they were munching, a voice from the floor piped up, 'Don't forget me.'

Paton and Jack looked round the table, mystified by the disembodied voice.

'Who was that?' asked Paton, looking under the table.

'Oh, we forgot Mr Puzzle,' said Hetty, lifting the weasel on to the table. 'There was so much to tell you, we left him out. I'm so sorry, Mr Puzzle.'

'Good afternoon!' Mr Puzzle made a sort of bow in Paton's direction. 'My name is Peregrine Puzzle, I am choirmaster at Ludgarth Hall School. At least, I was.'

Paton Yewbeam was seldom surprised by anything, but now his mouth hung open and his black eyebrows drew together in a frown of disbelief.

Mr Silk asked gently, 'Did *she* do this to you, Mr Puzzle?'

The weasel sighed. 'She did. I never imagined her sorcery could be so wicked, and so powerful.'

'Oh, she can do worse,' said Jack. 'Do have a scone, Mr Puzzle. You're welcome to stay here as long as, well . . .'

'As long as you like,' said Sadie. 'We'll be happy to have your company, even if you're always a weasel.'

'I hope that won't be the case,' said Mr Puzzle, looking downcast for a moment. 'But you're very kind. Thank you.' He helped himself to a scone. 'I always feel sleepy after a meal,' he said when he had swallowed a large chunk, and in no time at all he had finished the scone, curled himself up on the table and fallen asleep.

'There's no question of moving him, I suppose?' said Mr Silk, looking at the sleeping weasel.

The children smiled and Sadie said, 'It wouldn't be fair. He saved our lives, you know.'

Hetty said that she must be off to see her father, who would want to know everything there was to know. 'But I'll be back,' she said. 'There's still a cloak to be found.'

As soon as she had gone Gabriel and Sadie took turns in describing everything that had happened in Ludgarth, as accurately as they could manage. Gabriel was rather disappointed that his uncle and Paton weren't more horrified or amazed by the story.

'You mustn't think we're not impressed,' said Paton, 'but we've been through some extraordinary times ourselves.'

Gabriel remembered his friend Charlie's terrible battles with sinister relations. 'But I don't suppose you've ever met a phantom Sleeper,' he said, hopefully.

Paton laughed. 'Never,' he agreed.

Talk of phantom Sleepers reminded Paton that he had made a discovery. 'We haven't been idling away here, while you were fighting sorcery,' he told Gabriel.

'No. We've been going through those books,' Uncle Jack indicated the pile on the counter. 'Every day and every night. I would have given up, but Paton knew there was more to find, and he was right.

Gabriel sat up. 'What did you find?' he asked.

Paton retrieved one of his tomes. He placed it on the table, taking care not to disturb the weasel. Turning the long, rustling pages he eventually came to a place where a blue velvet ribbon had been inserted.

Paton ran his finger down the page. 'Here it is,' he said. 'I'll have to translate, this Old English is not always clear, as you know. However, what it states, more or less, is that two of the phantom Sleepers came from a noble family. They lived in a castle way up in the north-east. One winter night the castle was attacked from the sea.' Paton glanced up briefly. 'Probably by Vikings. They slaughtered the servants, the soldiers, the count and countess and all their children, except for two – the eldest son and the youngest daughter. Gold, silver and jewels were stolen, the castle was torched and the raiders sailed away.'

Everyone in the room remained silent, looking at Paton, and waiting breathlessly for more of the story.

'The two surviving children,' went on Paton, 'lay under the bodies, waiting to be burned alive. And then, snow came. Thick and fierce, it covered the castle and put out the flames.'

'And then?' asked Gabriel.

Paton pushed his reading glasses back up his nose and resumed his reading. 'The children, Etzel and Elissa, left their ruined home and walked for many miles. It is believed that they had heard of the Red King and were seeking his protection.' Keeping his finger on the page, Paton looked at his audience. 'By now the king was extremely old, but because of the cloak he was untouched by age. His family were all gone, of course, they had long ago scattered into the wide world. The king had abandoned his castle, and now held a small court in the forest.'

Sadie asked, 'So Etzel and Elissa found the Red King in the forest?'

'The king welcomed them,' said Paton, 'and they lived at his court for five years.' He returned to the book. 'Etzel was the king's page, Elissa his seamstress.

Erebus, the scribe, was told to instruct them in reading and writing, something they could not do when they arrived. Etzel, in particular, was a fast learner, and soon knew more than Erebus could teach him. It was quite clear that the newcomers were the king's favourites, and Erebus became very jealous.'

'Because Etzel was clever?' asked Sadie.

Paton speculated that it might have been because Etzel was a count. 'They would argue constantly,' he said, finding his place on the page. 'Once, Erebus whipped the boy, and was severely reprimanded by the king, thus inflaming the scribe's hatred of the young count even further.'

Sadie grimaced. 'How unfair.'

'But not unusual,' her father remarked.

'One winter,' Paton continued, 'a deadly malady came to trouble the court. Many died, but the king, in spite of his marvellous magic, was unable to help them. Etzel became sick, and then Elissa. Erebus blamed them for sneezing at the table, for soon he too became sick.' Paton closed the book and stared at his audience. His gaze came to rest on Gabriel, and a shiver tightened every nerve in Gabriel's body. He had never seen such intensity in Paton's deep, dark eyes.

'And so,' went on Paton, 'the king, unable to save his dying servants, made a promise. He would find a way to wake them if ever his cloak was stolen from the chosen Keepers.' He uttered a quick 'huh!' and then said, 'I imagine his only reason for waking Erebus was because of the scribe's dogged determination.'

'But why the cloak?' asked Gabriel. 'Why not wake the servants for another reason?'

Paton looked sternly at him. 'You know very well, Gabriel, you of all people.'

Gabriel looked away from the penetrating dark eyes.

'You have felt them, haven't you?' said Paton. 'The tears of creatures that have long disappeared from the world, the dew from flowers that we shall never see, all caught in the frail web of the last moon spider, and all there in the Red King's cloak: our link with the past, a bond that must never be lost, or broken.'

'Yes,' said Gabriel quietly. 'I have felt them.'

Paton laid his hand on the book in front of him. 'In the very first of these ancient books, we read of the jinni who gave the web to the Red King's mother, a thousand years ago, and how the young king turned the web into an enchanted cloak.'

'And then came to Britain,' said Gabriel. 'But . . . but if the king was powerful enough to make sure the phantoms would wake, how come he couldn't save their lives?'

Paton raised his impressive eyebrows. 'Who

knows, Gabriel? There is sometimes no logic to magic, and it was a very long time ago. But perhaps the king had no time to find a cure for such a deadly sickness, and yet he was certain that, one day, he would learn how to wake them.'

'Three phantom Sleepers,' Mr Silk mused, 'brings us right back to the cloak.'

Gabriel, still dazed from Paton Yewbeam's reading, found himself thinking of the phantoms' last strange battle. 'Etzel, Count of Orestone,' he murmured, 'that's what Erebus called him.'

Paton frowned. 'Now, where did I see that name? It's not in the passage I've just read.'

Mr Silk removed his spectacles and rubbed his weary eyes. 'Not another night of reading,' he implored, 'I've got a table to finish before the end of the week.'

Paton assured him that there was no need for him to do any more reading. 'I'm sure I can find the place without your help,' he said.

Sadie had another idea. She ran to the computer in the sitting room and put in the name Orestone into an internet search. Then, just for good measure, she added the word 'castle'. Her cry of delight brought Gabriel running to her side.

'What is it? What have you found?'

'Look!' Sadie pointed at the screen.

Gabriel saw fishing boats moored in a small harbour. A rough causeway led from the shore to a ruined castle on a rocky island. Some of the walls had fallen away, but a square tower remained. Seabirds perched on the broken ramparts, and waves foamed against the weed-strewn cliffs. At the bottom of the screen a short paragraph informed them that Castle Orestone had been gutted several hundred years ago, and was the site of a terrible massacre. The castle was now home to gulls and guillemots, and could only be reached at low tide, or by boat.

'It's *so* beautiful,' Sadie murmured.

'*Was* beautiful,' Gabriel remarked. 'Looks more like a heap of rubble now.'

'How can you say that?' Sadie said fiercely. 'It was Etzel's home.'

Gabriel retreated to the kitchen. 'We found the phantoms' castle,' he told his uncle and Paton. 'It's a ruin. And I don't see how it can help us to find the cloak.'

'Something might occur.' Paton patted his scalp. 'I'll think on it.'

'Well, I've got a leg to finish,' said Jack. 'Come and give me an opinion.'

Paton went dutifully into the workshop, but Gabriel declined. Mr Puzzle was still asleep so, when Sadie had finished looking at the castle on the internet,

Gabriel joined her in a walk around the town.

On their return, the children cooked sausages, chips and peas for everyone, including Mr Puzzle. When they'd eaten and washed up Sadie put a large cushion on the table as a bed for Mr Puzzle. Paton slept on the sofa in the sitting room.

After their escape from Ludgarth Hall and the long journey home, the children were happy to make their way up to bed. Thoughts of the cloak slipped away from Gabriel's weary mind, he even forgot about Erebus. As soon as he closed his eyes, he was asleep.

It was not the same for Sadie. Long after the house had fallen silent, she lay awake. Her eyes wide, she filled the darkness with images of a prince in gold and green. Behind him stood a castle, its pale sunlit walls dappled with shadows of birds in flight.

A ripple of green light stole across the ceiling, and Sadie lifted her head. The patch of light widened and intensified. Now Sadie was sitting bolt upright. Slipping out of bed, she crept to the window and looked out.

The garden was free of snow but the pale green mist that filled it was not the colour of grass. Sadie tiptoed downstairs and cautiously opened the front door. Etzel stood before her. The grey shroud covered his tunic and he wore his hood.

'Count Etzel,' Sadie whispered. 'Why have

you come?'

''Tis my duty til the cloak be found.'

He had changed since she last saw him. Now his face looked more than pale, it was almost translucent. He had stayed too long in the world.

'Let the Keeper find his way,' she said. 'He won't be alone.'

Etzel slowly shook his head. 'I must remain in the Keeper's company.'

Sadie couldn't bear to think of Etzel's handsome face decaying in the air. What if he began to look like Erebus? 'Leave the Keeper,' she said. 'You should go back . . .' She couldn't bring herself to mention his tomb.

Etzel gazed up at the stars. She wanted to touch his cheek, but took his hand instead. How cool it was, the skin so thin it moved over his bones like silk. 'Oh, Etzel,' she said. 'It's not good for you to stay.'

'Say-dee,' he said with a sigh, and it was *he* who touched *her* cheek. 'Another purpose keeps me here.'

She would remember that touch until she was very old. 'What purpose?' she asked.

'I have not seen my sister since she left the world, but I must, just once. She was everything to me, and I to her. I carried her on my shoulders through the snow.' His large eyes filled with glistening tears. 'She is in the world again.'

Sadie thought of the castle in flames, covered by falling snow. 'It has stopped snowing,' she said. 'If Elissa brought the snow, does that mean that she has gone back now?'

'She stays.' Etzel's form began to fade. ''Tis my belief . . . the cloak . . . she is the strongest of us all . . .' His words, spoken in a whisper, now made no sound at all. His pale lips moved and then he vanished.

Sadie stood a moment watching the green mist disappear.

She knew what Gabriel had to do.

CHAPTER FIFTEEN
Following the Snow

Gabriel wasn't too happy about the way Sadie woke him up. She practically hauled him upright, then waved a cup of tea under his nose. The curtains were open but it was still dark outside.

'It's late!' Sadie informed him.

'Already?' mumbled Gabriel.

Sadie knelt on his bed and put her face very close to his. 'The cloak, Gabe. You haven't forgotten, have you?' She wore a look of barely contained excitement.

'Course not.' Gabriel took the tea and sipped it. 'But we need time to gather our thoughts. I mean, where do we look next?'

Sadie sat back. Her eyes were sparkling and her loosened hair rippled to her waist, like an untidy cloak. 'We look for snow,' she said, somewhat triumphantly.

Gabriel was baffled. 'Snow?'

'Yes!' Sadie bounced off the bed. 'The snow has

gone. I think Elissa brought the snow. We might not have seen her, but she's awake. I think that means that Elissa is somewhere else now. She has taken the snow, and the cloak.'

Gabriel frowned. 'How do you know that Elissa has the cloak?'

'Oh, Gabe, it's obvious. Think about it. The girl's voice in the snow, when the cloak was taken. It sounded like old English, remember? "Not thine," it said.'

Comprehension slowly dawned in Gabriel's weary head. 'Sadie, you're a genius. And I'm the stupidest person you've probably ever met.'

'You've had a tough time,' Sadie said generously. 'So come on, get dressed. We have to find the snow.'

Gabriel had another thought. 'Suppose Elissa has taken the cloak back to wherever she came from? Perhaps the phantoms don't trust us any more, and they've decided to remove it forever.'

'Elissa is still in the world,' Sadie told him. 'Etzel said so.'

'Etzel? Have you seen him, then?'

'Last night. Just for a moment.' She laid a hand briefly against her cheek, and then quickly left the room.

Gabriel stared after her, wondering why Etzel had appeared to Sadie and no one else. By the time he got down to the kitchen a snowfall had been located.

'Extraordinary,' said Paton Yewbeam, reaching for a third piece of toast. 'I've never known snow fall in one small place, while the rest of the country is basking in winter sun.'

'A phenomenon,' Jack agreed.

Gabriel pulled out a chair and helped himself to cereal. 'So where is it then, this snowfall?'

'In the north-east!' Sadie announced. 'It was on the internet forecast *and* the radio. Snow has been seen in tiny patches, travelling north.'

'Are we going somewhere?' Gabriel asked Sadie.

'Of course,' she said. 'To Brimscud. Hetty will be here any minute. She's been amazing. Our rooms are booked at a B&B. Her dad is checking the Land Rover and filling the tank, and Hetty's making food.'

It took a moment for Gabriel to absorb all of this. Eventually, he said, 'Brimscud, isn't that where . . .?

'Orestone Castle,' Paton said dryly. 'The village at the end of the causeway. He leaned across the table and looked solemnly into Gabriel's eyes. 'Elissa is awake. The snow. Elissa might be a child, but she is, perhaps, the most powerful phantom of all. I don't know why it didn't occur to any of us before. It's lucky one of us was on the ball.' He grinned at Sadie.

'It's still snowing there,' Jack added. 'The castle is completely covered.'

The doorbell rang and Jack left the room, saying, 'Better get your bags packed, children. That'll be Hetty.'

Gabriel hadn't seen his uncle looking so buoyant for a long time. He sounded hopeful, as if he'd begun to believe in something again.

Jack opened the door to Hetty just as the children were running upstairs. Gabriel, who hadn't finished his breakfast, began to hiccough.

'Five minutes, kids,' called Hetty. 'It's another long drive. Low tide will be at eight o'clock tomorrow morning. Hold your breath and count to five, Gabriel. It'll stop your hiccoughs.'

She was still in the hall when the children came down again, their bags unzipped and so hastily packed that sleeves and socks were still hanging out.

'We'll tidy those up in the car,' said Hetty, leading the way up the path.

Paton and Jack stood in the open doorway calling, 'Goodbye! Good luck! Phone us!'

Just as Gabriel was about to climb into the Land Rover, Paton's deep voice rang across the garden. 'Gabriel, the cloak is your ally. If it falls into the wrong hands it will fight back.' Almost as an afterthought, he added quietly, 'It can punish most horribly.'

'OK.' Gabriel gave a wave and jumped into the car. But as they drove away from The Carpenter's

Cabin, he wondered what he was supposed to do with such an unexpected warning.

It was a long journey, just as Hetty had predicted. They had two stops for water, a visit to the toilets and for Hetty to have fresh coffee, but she'd provided enough food to last for at least two days. Now and again she would catch sight of a sleek silver sports car in her rear-view mirror. It seemed to be going in the same direction, but she thought nothing of it.

They arrived in Brimscud in the late afternoon. It was already dark, but they could hear waves slapping the wooden fishing boats, and the sound of sheets rattling against the metal masts.

The little house where they were to stay the night was warm and welcoming. Their landlady, Mrs McKuddy, white-haired and wind-tanned, chattered away about the recent snowfall.

'The boats can't go out,' she said, 'with the air all white with snow. No visibility at all. It might be better by morning, though.'

She settled them by the fire, curious to know what had brought them to Brimscud in such weather.

Hetty was ready with her answer. 'We're on our way to see friends who find it difficult to travel.'

'Elderly, are they?' asked Mrs McKuddy.

'Very,' said Sadie. She considered this to be true.

'Ah, you're good people,' said the landlady. 'Some

young folk, these days, they're not so kind.'

Hetty asked if they could see where they were to sleep, and Mrs McKuddy led them up to the two guest rooms. Hetty and Sadie were to share, but Gabriel had a room to himself. He looked around it, at once feeling very at home. The walls were covered in leaf-patterned paper, and there was a small fireplace, with a decorated iron frame.

Gabriel put his bag beside the bed and went to the window. He could hardly believe his luck, for there, not far from the house, was the beginning of the causeway. He half-closed his eyes and stared at the great flat stones leading through the water. But no matter how hard he stared, he couldn't see more than a few metres. Darkness swallowed any view he might have had of the castle.

Snowflakes fluttered lightly now, they didn't settle. Gabriel fixed his gaze on a point in the distance where he thought the castle might lie. Tomorrow they would be there, and if the cloak were not found in that ancient ruin, then it might be lost forever. It was their last chance.

After a hearty fish supper beside the fire, the travellers were ready for bed. At the top of the stairs they bid each other goodnight. Even Hetty was aware of the tension in the air. Something momentous and final was going to occur. 'Sleep well, Gabriel,' she said.

Sadie was about to follow Hetty into their room when Gabriel held her back.

She turned and looked at him, a little anxiously.

'Tomorrow,' said Gabriel, 'as soon as it's light.'

Sadie gave him a secretive sort of smile. 'Tomorrow,' she said.

In spite of their restless excitement at what lay ahead the three travellers slept deeply.

'Sea air and fresh fish,' said Mrs McKuddy next morning, pleased to hear her guests had enjoyed their stay. 'Will you be travelling on, now?'

'We thought we'd take a little walk round the harbour,' said Hetty.

'It's a bit quiet this time of year,' said their landlady. 'Winter's not the best time. But you're welcome to leave your bags here while you wander.'

They thanked her, packed their bags and left them by the front door. When they stepped outside the children's gaze was immediately drawn towards the castle. The rocks beneath it looked higher than they had imagined, and the causeway much longer. But there was a reassuring chain-link rail, running between posts along one side of the stones.

Hetty was frowning at the sky. A line of dark, broken clouds was streaming towards them from the horizon. 'A storm,' she said. 'I don't like the look of it.'

'Let's go while we can, then,' said Gabriel.

A pale sun showed through the drifting snowflakes, giving the waves a light sparkle. The causeway, when they reached it, was firm and dry. The tide was out and the great stone structure stood well above the waves.

The causeway was wide enough for three to walk together, but they decided to go in single file, each of them holding to the chain railing. Gabriel led the way, Hetty came last. Ahead of them rose the castle. Even the tower was covered in snow and ice, and the great ruin resembled a mountain rather than a castle.

Step by step they drew closer. Gabriel's heart began to thump. He could hear Sadie's breath getting faster, and Hetty's walking boots thudding on the stones. None of them spoke.

They were halfway there when the breeze sharpened and in a second became a howling wind. Astonished by the sudden blast, they reeled back against the rail, grasping it with both hands. Gabriel saw that Hetty was some way behind them. She waved, and the very next moment, a great torrent of water came out of nowhere. It towered above the causeway like some angry giant before coming down smack between Hetty and the children.

Hetty attempted to walk across the stream of

water from the receding wave, but as soon as she did so another rose beside her and she backed away, still clinging to the railing.

'Run, children', she called. 'As fast as you can. Run for the island.'

How could they run? The sea boiled against the causeway, swelling and falling. A dangerous grumbling sound echoed up to them from deep below the water.

'We're not wanted here,' Sadie cried through the wind. 'It's as if they're trying to stop us.'

'Who?' said Gabriel. Not the phantoms, he thought.

Moving slowly, hand over hand, they battled through the wild weather until they reached the island. But another hazard awaited them. The steps up to the castle were slippery with ice. Gabriel set his foot on the first step.

'Can't stop now,' he said. 'Come on, Sadie!' Yesterday the cloak had seemed as distant as ever, but now, in this remote and dangerous place, he felt quite sure that it was close.

They had to climb on all fours, their feet sliding on the frozen seaweed. Eventually, Gabriel pulled himself to the top and tugged Sadie up beside him.

They waited a moment to catch their breath. The castle tower was only a few feet away. The children looked at each other. Without saying a word, Gabriel took his cousin's hand again.

Together they walked up to the great arched entrance. Sadie glanced down at the sea, just once, and wished she hadn't. The rocks beneath looked cruel today, with wild sea foam sweeping over them.

Snow began to fall again, very gently; soft feathers of snow that danced in the air with an almost magical glitter.

With hands clasped tight the cousins walked under the great arch, through the tower and out into an open courtyard. Small patches of grass showed in the snow, and high above, the remaining ramparts stood stark against the wintry sky. It was so quiet. The floating crystals made no sound at all.

Images of the fire crept into their thoughts. The leaping flames, the cries and sounds of battle, and then the falling snow and the two who were left alive. Great stones lay scattered on the ground, where they had tumbled from the walls.

They stepped closer to the centre, searching the icy ramparts for any sign of a girl holding a red cloak. Would she be dressed in a grey shroud? Gabriel wondered.

CHAPTER SIXTEEN
Elissa

'Is she here?' Sadie whispered. 'Elissa?'

'Yes,' said Gabriel. 'I'm sure.'

There was a movement on the other side of the courtyard. The children tensed as the figure came towards them. It was tall, not the girl they had expected. This person was much older. Her hair was grey and stiff, the hem of her dress covered her ankles and she wore a long cape of black fur.

It was the sorceress.

Sadie's scream died in her throat. Gabriel clutched her hand so fiercely she couldn't tell which fingers were hers.

A dreadful laugh echoed round the walls. 'Stupid children,' called the sorceress. 'Didn't you guess that I would follow you?' The awful laugh came again. 'Oh, the cloak is here, I can smell it. But it's not for you, Keeper.'

Every word she spoke brought her closer to them.

The children stepped away from her, back and back, before she could bring those wicked fingers from beneath her cape.

Sadie put her free hand under her scarf and touched the obsidian star.

The sorceress sneered, 'Your little piece of luck might save you from a spell, Sadie Silk, but it won't save you from the sea.'

They were now beneath the arch again, a few steps behind them lay a deadly fall into the water. And no one would know the truth. They would just be two foolish children who should never have been there.

There is something I can do, thought Gabriel. A phantom Sleeper brought me here. He searched his memory for Etzel's words. Erebus to lead, Etzel to accompany and Elissa to . . .? What was Elissa's role? Fear and confusion clouded Gabriel's mind. He couldn't think, couldn't remember.

As the sorceress lifted her deadly fingers it suddenly came to him – Elissa was to answer.

'Elissa!' Gabriel cried. 'Elissa, answer us!'

Momentarily distracted, the sorceress lowered her hand, and Sadie called, 'Elissa! Elissa! Help us!'

From high on the ramparts there came a call, a girl's voice. It was almost as though she were singing. 'Elissa hears. Elissa answers.'

They could see her now, a small figure in white,

her grey shroud thrown back, her long hair blowing free. A red garment lay across her raised arms. She held it over the low rampart wall and let it drop.

How slowly it fell, drifting gently through the white air.

The sorceress gave a shout of triumph and lifted her arms. The cloak was coming towards her, soon it would be hers. 'Come to me! Come to me!' she cried.

Gabriel and Sadie watched helplessly. Was this Elissa's answer? This cruel trick?

Sadie whispered, 'Believe in her, Gabriel. Believe in Elissa. The cloak belongs to us.'

Gabriel looked at Sadie, the cloak still slowly falling. Sadie is a Silk, too, he thought. There are two of us, and we are children of the Red King. Elissa would always obey the king. She had taken it upon herself to save the cloak; she would only return it to the rightful Keeper. 'I believe,' he said aloud.

Even as he spoke, the cloak touched Cecily's eager hands, but it didn't fall into her waiting arms, instead it draped itself over her head. She wrestled with it for a moment, trying to pull it off, but it appeared to be too heavy for her. She fell to her knees, still tugging. Her voice could be heard, muffled and choking as she sank lower, beating against the heavy stuff that was now completely covering her.

Lower and lower. The sorceress dropped and

withered. A feeble moan came from beneath the cloak, and then the voice was silent.

'Where has she gone?' asked Sadie, her own voice hushed and fearful. For the cloak lay flat on the ground.

They looked round the courtyard, their eyes searching every corner. They scanned the great walls and stared at the fallen stones. Sadie ran out and studied the coarse grass that clung to the ground between the castle and the sea. She even stood at the very edge of the island and gazed down at the waves. They were calmer now. Seabirds bobbed on the swell, but there was nothing else.

Gabriel came and took her hand. He gently drew her away from the edge. 'It isn't her sorcery,' he told her. 'Remember what Paton said? "The cloak will fight back. It can punish most horribly." I think Cecily Fork is still there, Sadie.'

They went and stood on either side of the cloak. Gabriel took a deep breath, bent and lifted it up. Beneath was a long grey stone. There were streaks of dull steel at one end, like half-buried knives, and what might have been the imprint of an open mouth.

Sadie quickly stepped back. She looked into Gabriel's dark eyes and said, 'It's her.'

Gabriel looked away. He hugged the cloak, feeling the warmth of it on his chest, and was flooded with such happiness he had to close his eyes.

At that moment, far away in Ludgarth Hall, three previously silent sisters began to talk. Their throats were parched from being such a long time without chatter, but now they croaked and sang and laughed so much, their brother had to cover his ears. Then all four went running down the many staircases, past rooms of strangely quiet slow-moving people, and out into the cool, fresh air.

A boy, who, only a minute ago, had been a dog, watched the family run down the hill. He shrugged his shoulders, scratched the place where one of his dog ears had been and went in search of his brother.

In The Carpenter's Cabin, Jack Silk walked into his kitchen and found a stranger sitting in the middle of the table.

'Do forgive me,' said the man. 'I seem to be Peregrine Puzzle again. I don't usually sit on other people's tables. We met under rather different circumstances.'

'We did, indeed,' said Jack. He shook the man's hand, observing his very round, bright eyes. 'Will you excuse me for a moment? I believe something has happened.'

Jack ran to the front door. 'Paton, Paton,' he called. 'I hardly dare to hope, and yet I think, yes, I do definitely think . . .' He flung open the door, walked out and took in great lungfuls of air. 'I can breathe,' he shouted.

Paton Yewbeam watched his friend march down the path, open the gate and step into the street. 'It's Jack Silk,' he announced to anyone who cared to listen. 'I'm out in the world again!'

'Bravo!' called Paton.

Sadie and Gabriel gazed up at the ramparts. The snow had all but ceased, only a few flakes hovered in the air. Elissa was still there, high above them. She seemed to be smiling. They weren't sure if they should wave to her, but while they were wondering, a green mist began to form about the girl.

Sadie uttered a little cry. 'It's Etzel. He followed you.'

'And found his sister,' said Gabriel.

Etzel stood beside Elissa. He took her hand and made a little bow towards the children. 'I thank thee, Keeper,' he called. 'Live well.'

Elissa laid her head against her brother's chest and he held her tight, drawing his shroud about her. They faded very slowly, almost as though they were reluctant to leave the world.

The children waited until there was nothing left to see. The ramparts were empty, the sky a clear, icy blue. Seabirds swooped and called above them.

'Goodbye,' Sadie said quietly.

The wind had dropped and their descent on the slippery steps seemed easier than their climb. They had only gone a short distance across the causeway when Sadie stopped and looked back at the castle.

Gabriel let her dream for a moment, and then he said, 'Perhaps you'll never live in a castle, Sadie, but you'll always be the best cousin anyone could ever have.'

She didn't reply, but gave him the biggest smile she could manage. When she turned away from the castle, there was Hetty, running towards them, calling joyfully, her arms flung wide.

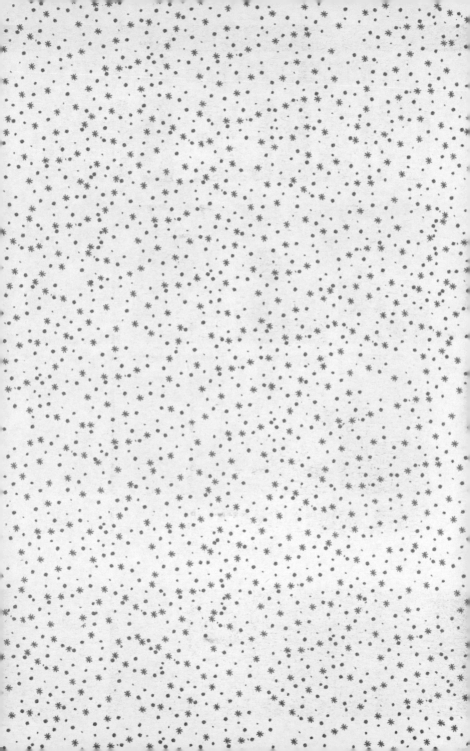